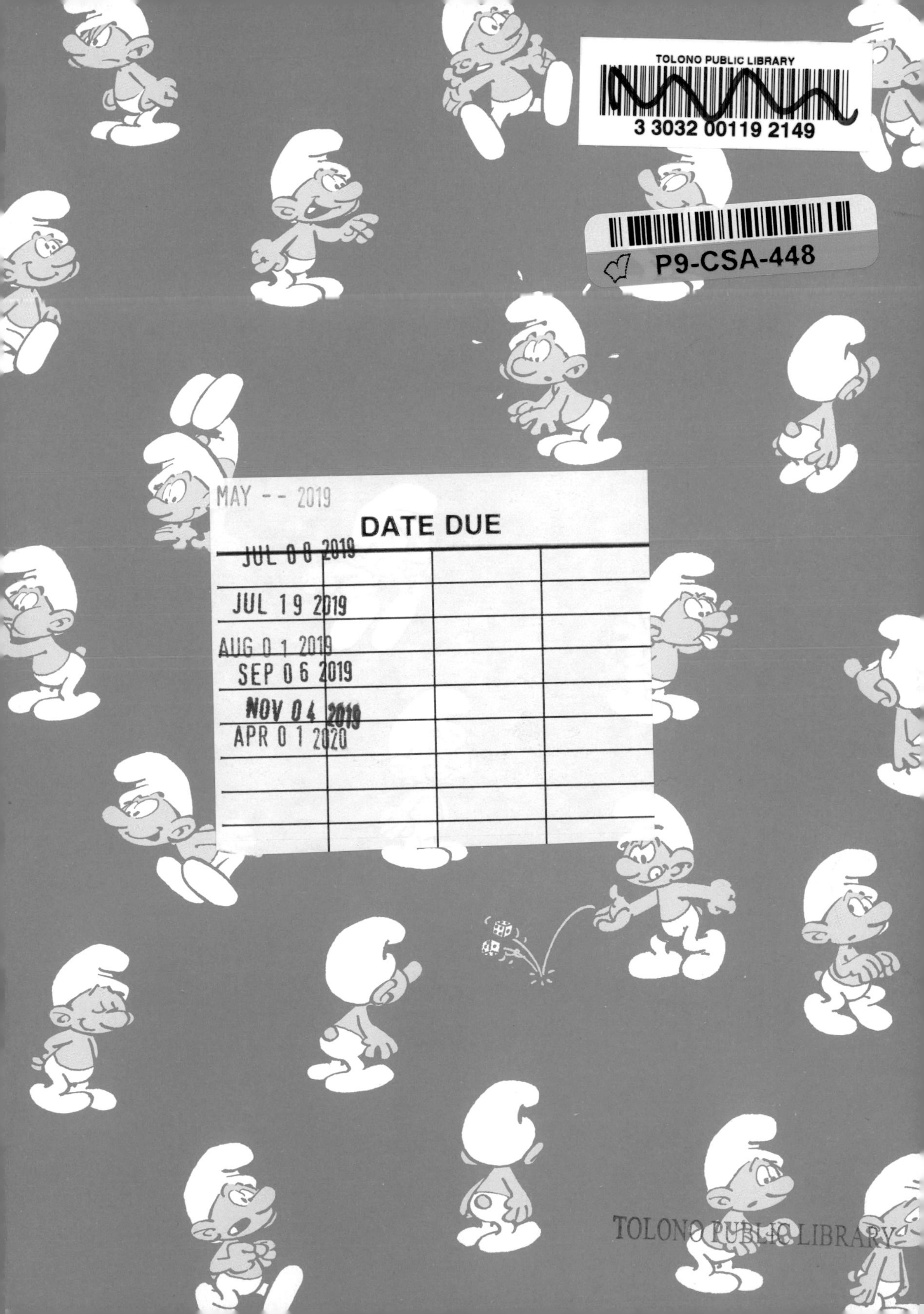

# THE G♠MBLING SMURFS

*Peyo*

A **SMURFS** GRAPHIC NOVEL BY *Peyo*

WITH THE COLLABORATION OF
LUC PARTHOENS AND THIERRY CULLIFORD – SCRIPT
LUDO BORECKI – ART
NINE CULLIFORD – COLOR

PAPERCUT**Z**™
NEW YORK

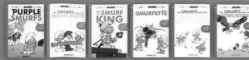

## SMURFS GRAPHIC NOVELS AVAILABLE FROM PAPERCUTZ™

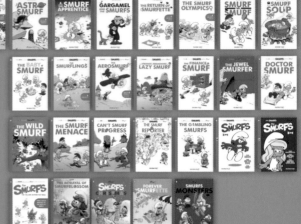

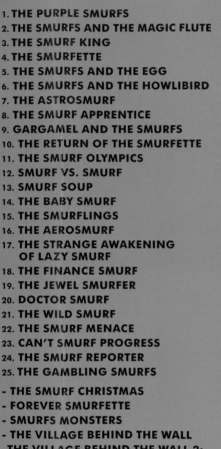

1. THE PURPLE SMURFS
2. THE SMURFS AND THE MAGIC FLUTE
3. THE SMURF KING
4. THE SMURFETTE
5. THE SMURFS AND THE EGG
6. THE SMURFS AND THE HOWLIBIRD
7. THE ASTROSMURF
8. THE SMURF APPRENTICE
9. GARGAMEL AND THE SMURFS
10. THE RETURN OF THE SMURFETTE
11. THE SMURF OLYMPICS
12. SMURF VS. SMURF
13. SMURF SOUP
14. THE BABY SMURF
15. THE SMURFLINGS
16. THE AEROSMURF
17. THE STRANGE AWAKENING OF LAZY SMURF
18. THE FINANCE SMURF
19. THE JEWEL SMURFER
20. DOCTOR SMURF
21. THE WILD SMURF
22. THE SMURF MENACE
23. CAN'T SMURF PROGRESS
24. THE SMURF REPORTER
25. THE GAMBLING SMURFS

- THE SMURF CHRISTMAS
- FOREVER SMURFETTE
- SMURFS MONSTERS
- THE VILLAGE BEHIND THE WALL
- THE VILLAGE BEHIND THE WALL 2: THE BETRAYAL OF SMURFBLOSSOM

THE SMURFS 3 IN 1 #1
THE SMURFS 3 IN 1 #2

THE SMURFS graphic novels are available in paperback for $5.99 each and in hardcover for $10.99 each, except for THE SMURFS #21-#25, and THE VILLAGE BEHIND THE WALL, which are $7.99 each in paperback and $12.99 each in hardcover, at booksellers everywhere. THE SMURFS 3 IN 1 #1-2 are in paperback only for $14.99 each. You can also order online at papercutz.com. Or call 1-800-886-1223, Monday through Friday, 9 – 5 EST. MC, Visa, and AmEx accepted. To order by mail, please add $5.00 for postage and handling for first book ordered, $1.00 for each additional book and make check payable to NBM Publishing. Send to: Papercutz, 160 Broadway, Suite 700, East Wing, New York, NY 10038.

THE SMURFS graphic novels are also available digitally wherever e-books are sold.

PAPERCUTZ.COM

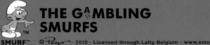

# THE GAMBLING SMURFS



"The Gambling Smurfs"
*BY PEYO*
*WITH THE COLLABORATION OF*
*LUC PARTHOENS AND THIERRY CULLIFORD FOR THE SCRIPT*
*LUDO BORECKI FOR ARTWORK*
*NINE CULLIFORD FOR COLOR.*

*"THE FLUTE SMURFERS"*
*BY PEYO*
*WITH THE COLLABORATION OF*
*LUC PARTHOENS AND THIERRY CULLIFORD FOR THE SCRIPT,*
*JEROEN DE CONINCK FOR ARTWORK,*
*NINE CULLIFORD FOR COLORS.*

Joe Johnson, *SMURFLATIONS*
Léa Zimmerman, *SMURFIC DESIGN*
Bryan Senka, *LETTERING SMURF ("THE GAMBLING SMURFS")*
Janice Chiang, *LETTERING SMURFETTE ("THE FLUTE SMURFERS")*
Matt. Murray, *SMURF CONSULTANT*
Karr Antunes, *SMURF INTERN*
Jeff Whitman, *MANAGING SMURF*
Jim Salicrup, *SMURF-IN-CHIEF*

*HARDCOVER EDITION ISBN: 978-1-5458-0149-9*
*PAPERBACK EDITION ISBN: 978-1-5458-0357-8*

*PRINTED IN KOREA MAY 2019*

Papercutz books may be purchased for business or promotional use. For information on bulk purchases please contact Macmillan Corporate and Premium Sales Department at (800) 221-7945 x5442.

*DISTRIBUTED BY MACMILLAN*
*FIRST PAPERCUTZ PRINTING*

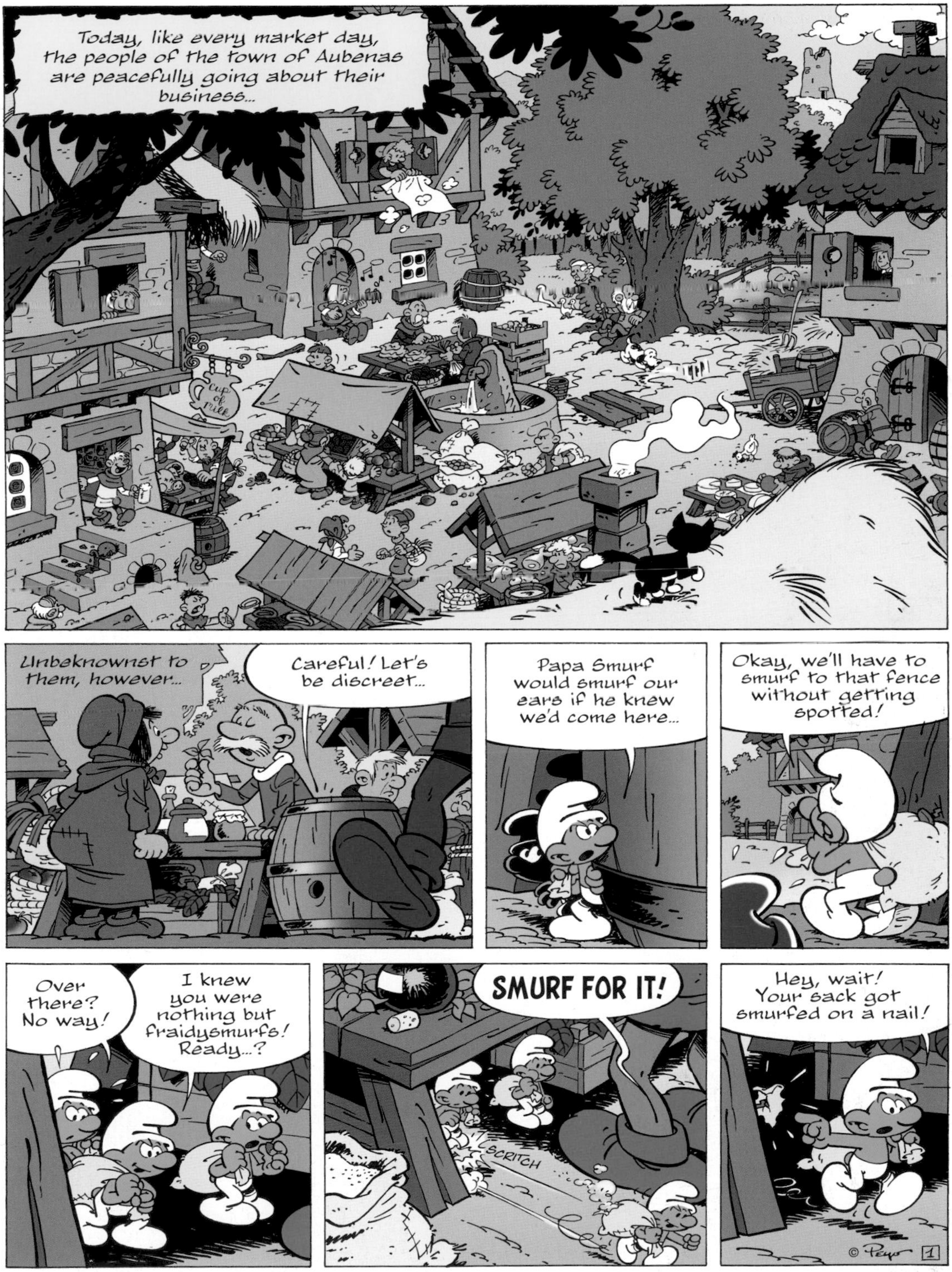
Today, like every market day, the people of the town of Aubenas are peacefully going about their business...
Cup of milk
Unbeknownst to them, however...
Careful! Let's be discreet...
Papa Smurf would smurf our ears if he knew we'd come here...
Okay, we'll have to smurf to that fence without getting spotted!
Over there? No way!
I knew you were nothing but fraidysmurfs! Ready...?
SMURF FOR IT!
SCRITCH
Hey, wait! Your sack got smurfed on a nail!
© Peyo
1

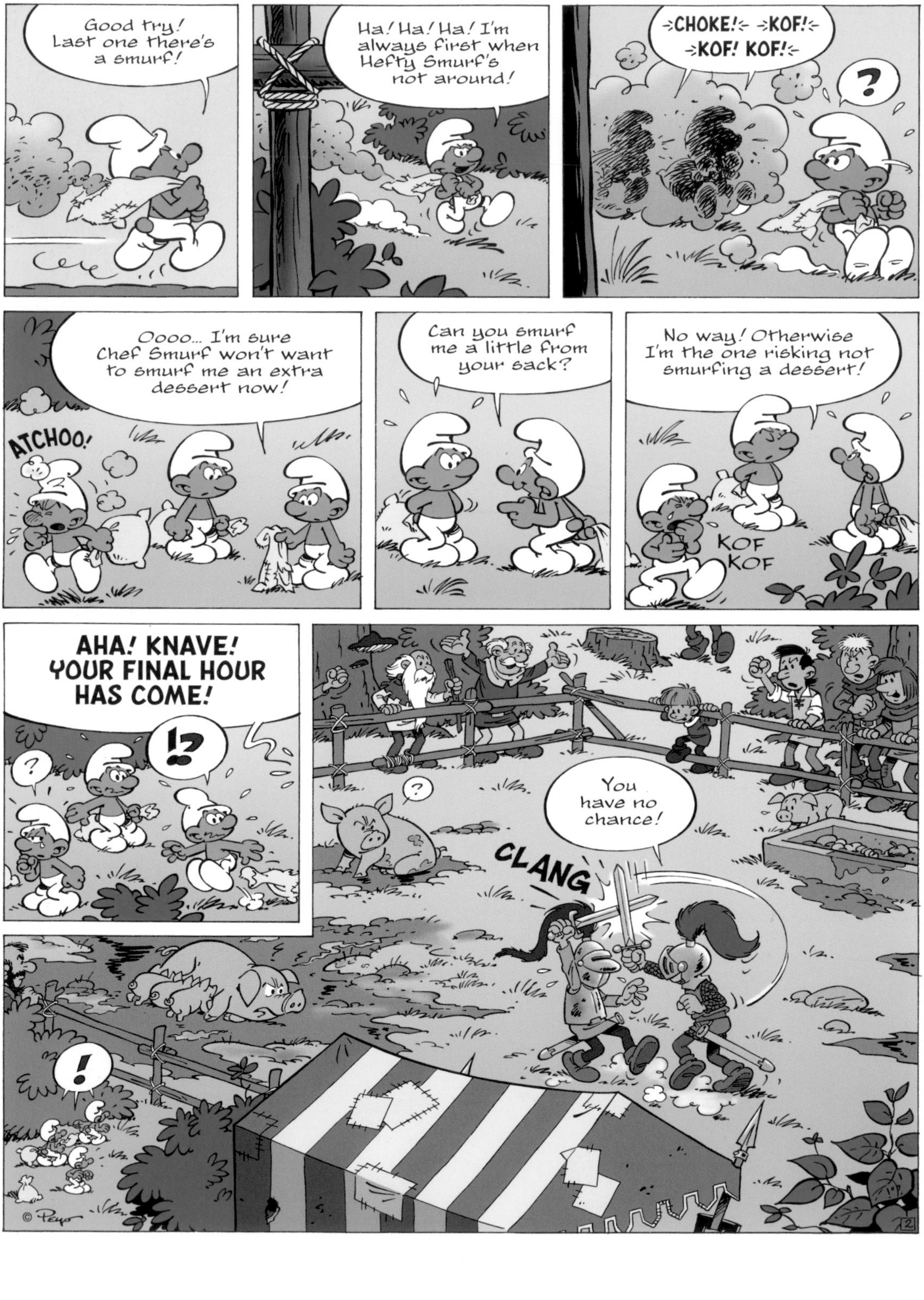

Good try! Last one there's a smurf!
Ha! Ha! Ha! I'm always first when Hefty Smurf's not around!
CHOKE! KOF! KOF! KOF!
?
Oooo... I'm sure Chef Smurf won't want to smurf me an extra dessert now!
ATCHOO!
Can you smurf me a little from your sack?
No way! Otherwise I'm the one risking not smurfing a dessert!
KOF KOF
AHA! KNAVE! YOUR FINAL HOUR HAS COME!
?
!?
?
You have no chance!
CLANG
!
© Peyo
2

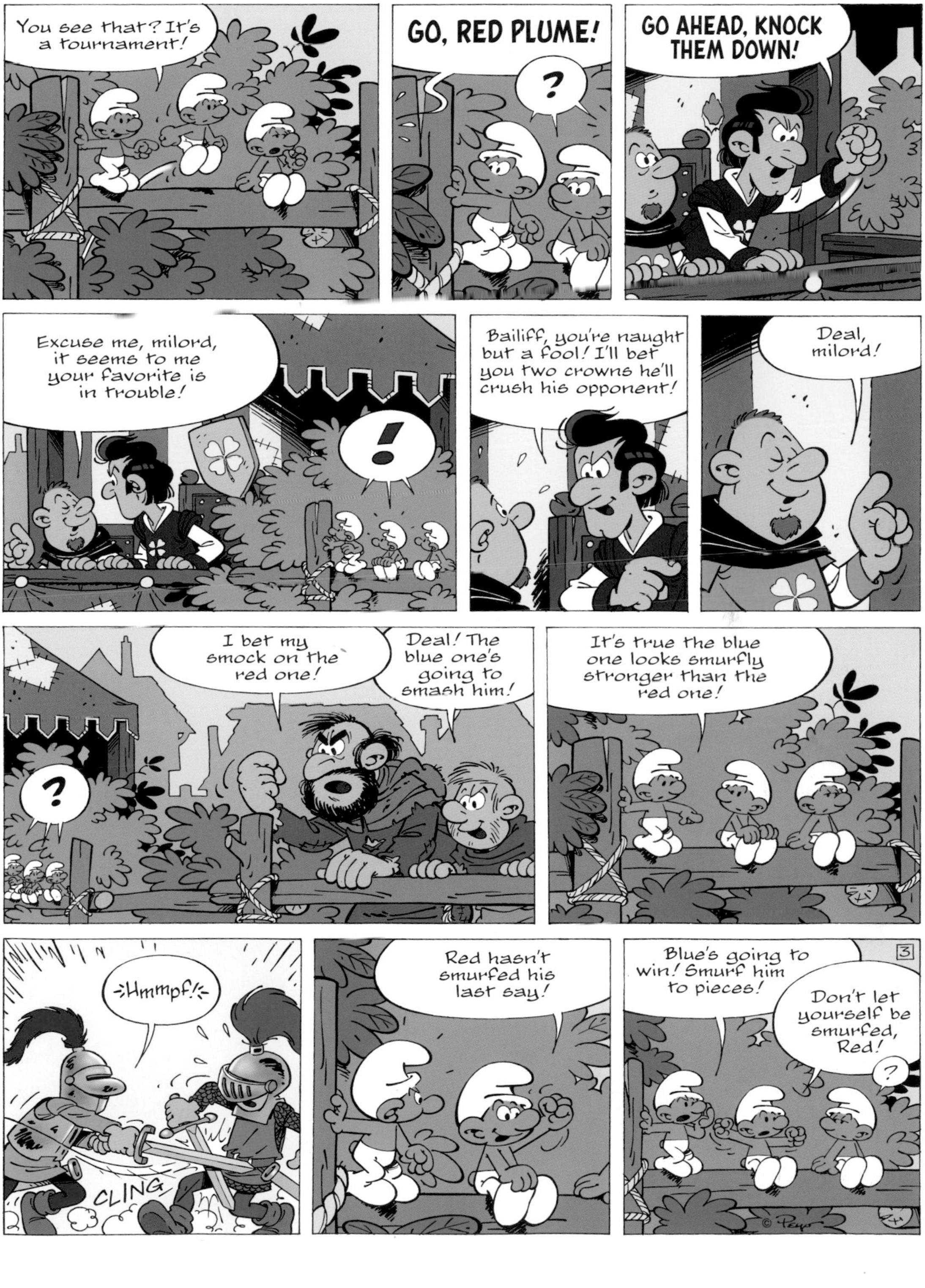

You see that? It's a tournament!
GO, RED PLUME!
?
GO AHEAD, KNOCK THEM DOWN!
Excuse me, milord, it seems to me your favorite is in trouble!
!
Bailiff, you're naught but a fool! I'll bet you two crowns he'll crush his opponent!
Deal, milord!
?
I bet my smock on the red one!
Deal! The blue one's going to smash him!
It's true the blue one looks smurfly stronger than the red one!
Hmmpf!
CLING
Red hasn't smurfed his last say!
3
Blue's going to win! Smurf him to pieces!
Don't let yourself be smurfed, Red!
?
© Peyo

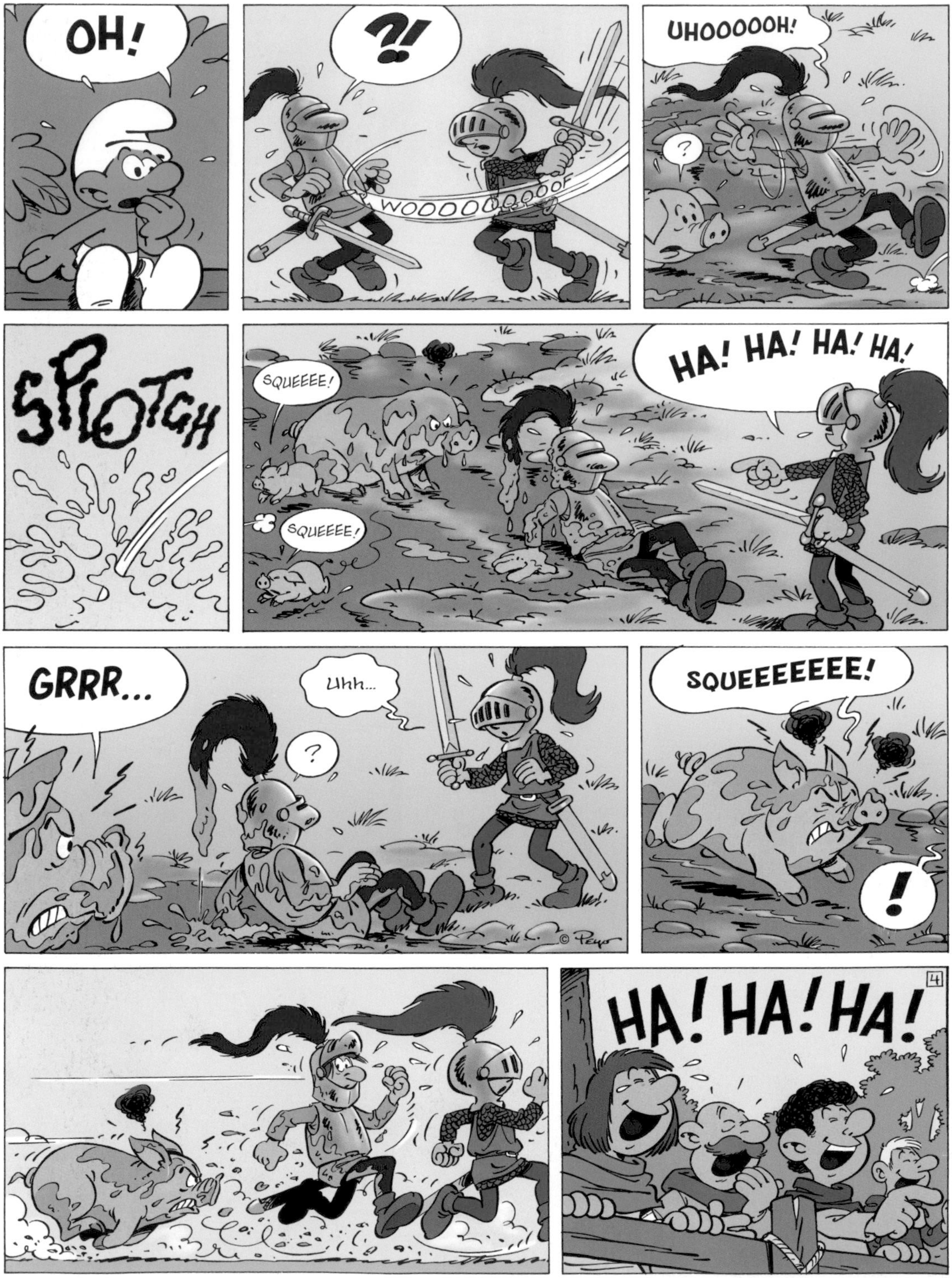
OH!
?!
WOOOOOOOOOOF
UHOOOOOH!
?
SPLOTCH
SQUEEEE!
SQUEEEE!
HA! HA! HA! HA!
GRRR...
Uhh...
?
© Peyo
SQUEEEEEEE!
!
4
HA! HA! HA!

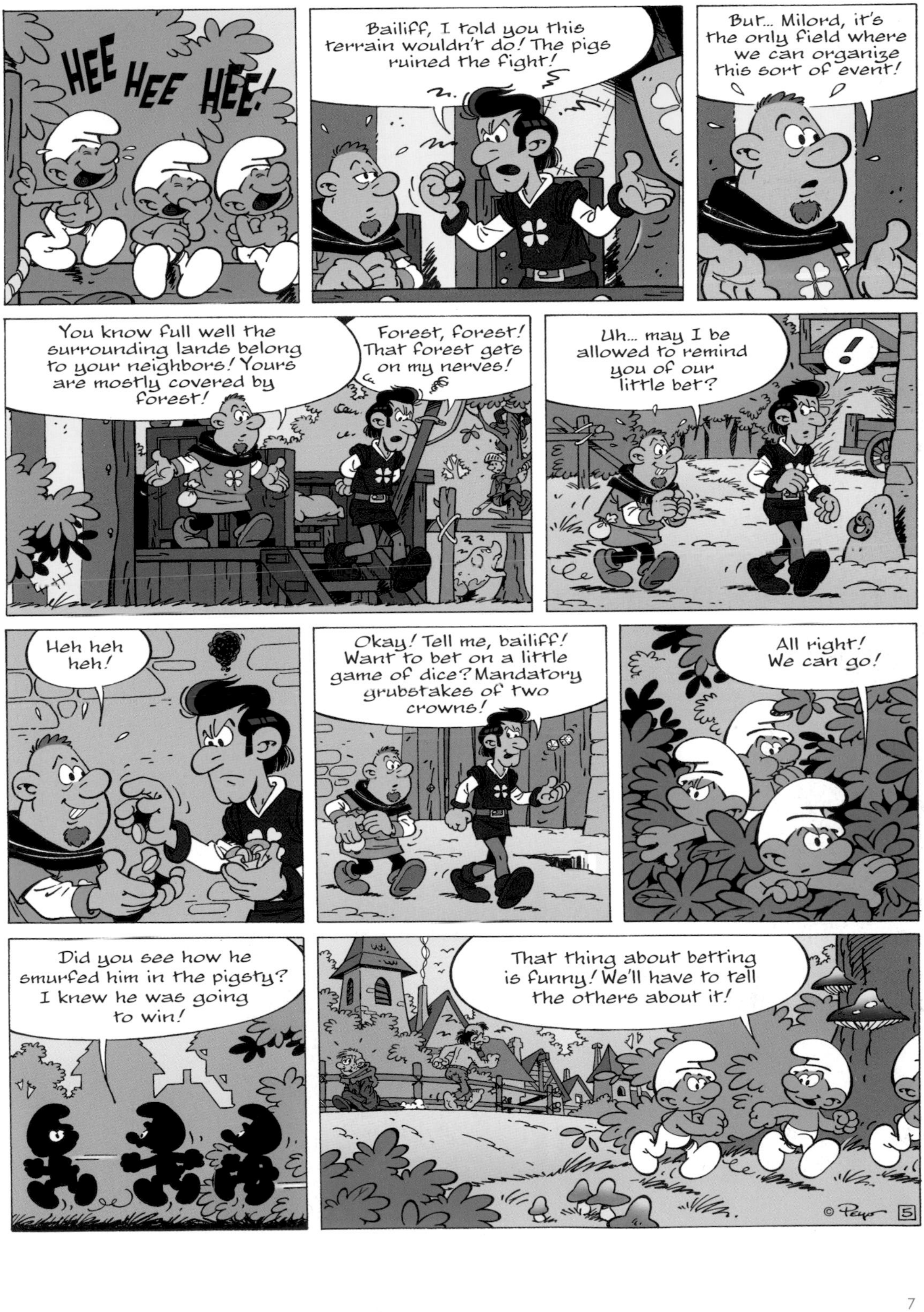

HEE HEE HEE!
Bailiff, I told you this terrain wouldn't do! The pigs ruined the fight!
But... Milord, it's the only field where we can organize this sort of event!
You know full well the surrounding lands belong to your neighbors! Yours are mostly covered by forest!
Forest, forest! That forest gets on my nerves!
Uh... may I be allowed to remind you of our little bet?
!
Heh heh heh!
Okay! Tell me, bailiff! Want to bet on a little game of dice? Mandatory grubstakes of two crowns!
All right! We can go!
Did you see how he smurfed him in the pigsty? I knew he was going to win!
That thing about betting is funny! We'll have to tell the others about it!
© Peyo
5

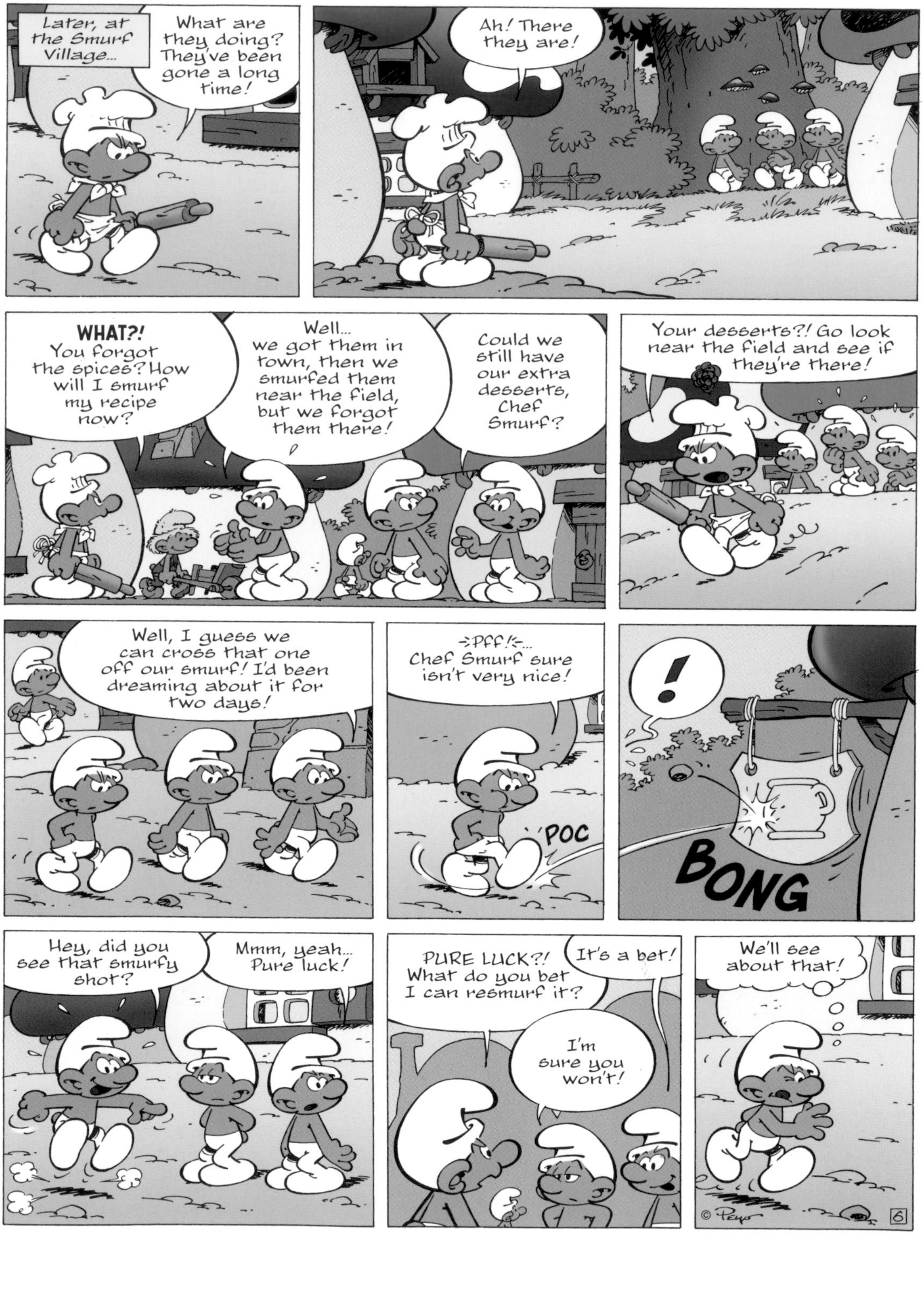

Later, at the Smurf Village...
What are they doing? They've been gone a long time!
Ah! There they are!
WHAT?! You forgot the spices? How will I smurf my recipe now?
Well... we got them in town, then we smurfed them near the field, but we forgot them there!
Could we still have our extra desserts, Chef Smurf?
Your desserts?! Go look near the field and see if they're there!
Well, I guess we can cross that one off our smurf! I'd been dreaming about it for two days!
-Pff!-... Chef Smurf sure isn't very nice!
POC
!
BONG
Hey, did you see that smurfy shot?
Mmm, yeah... Pure luck!
PURE LUCK?! What do you bet I can resmurf it?
It's a bet!
I'm sure you won't!
We'll see about that!
© Peyo
6

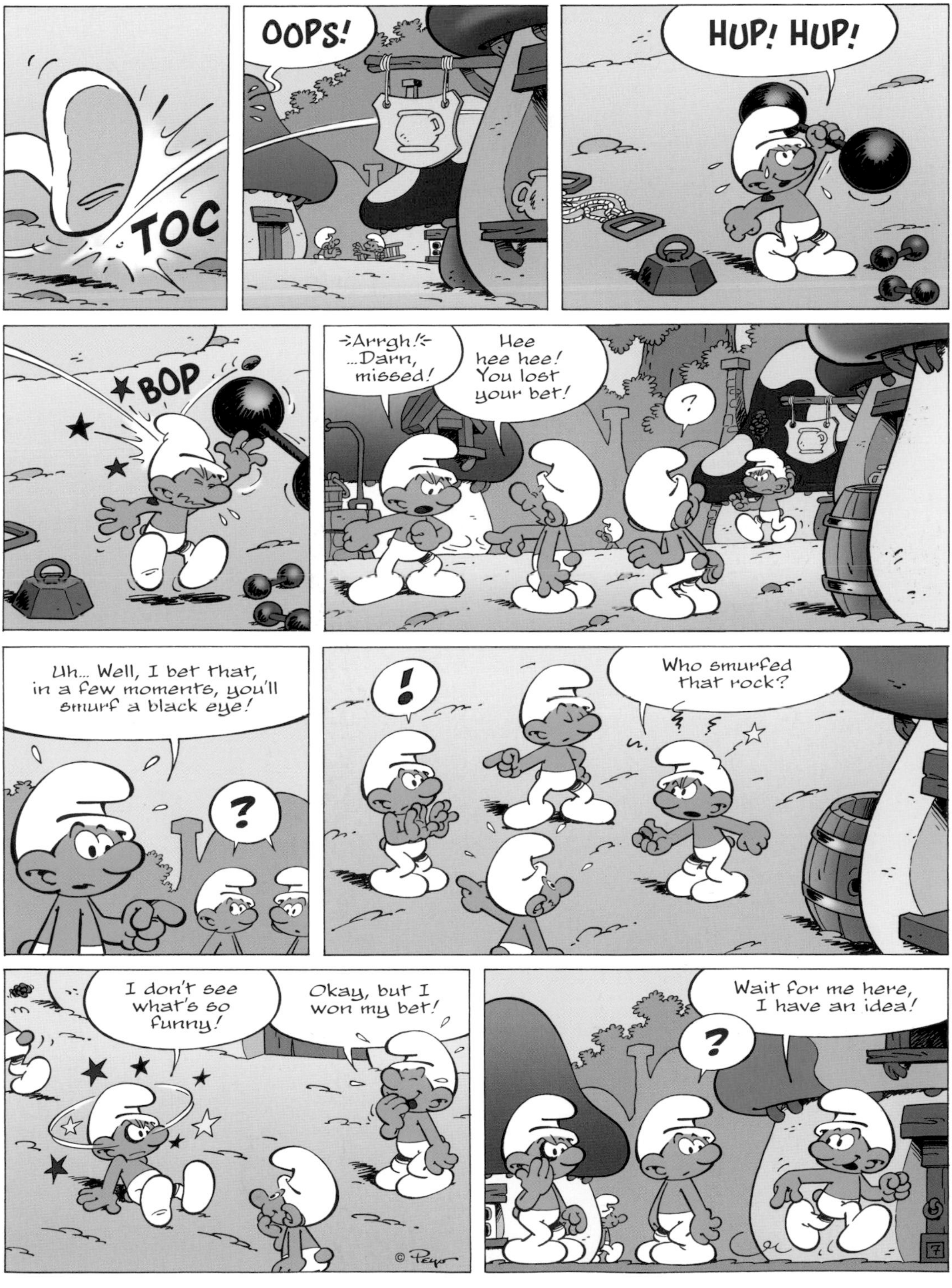

TOC
OOPS!
HUP! HUP!
BOP
Arrgh! ...Darn, missed!
Hee hee hee! You lost your bet!
?
Uh... Well, I bet that, in a few moments, you'll smurf a black eye!
?
!
Who smurfed that rock?
I don't see what's so funny!
Okay, but I won my bet!
© Peyo
?
Wait for me here, I have an idea!

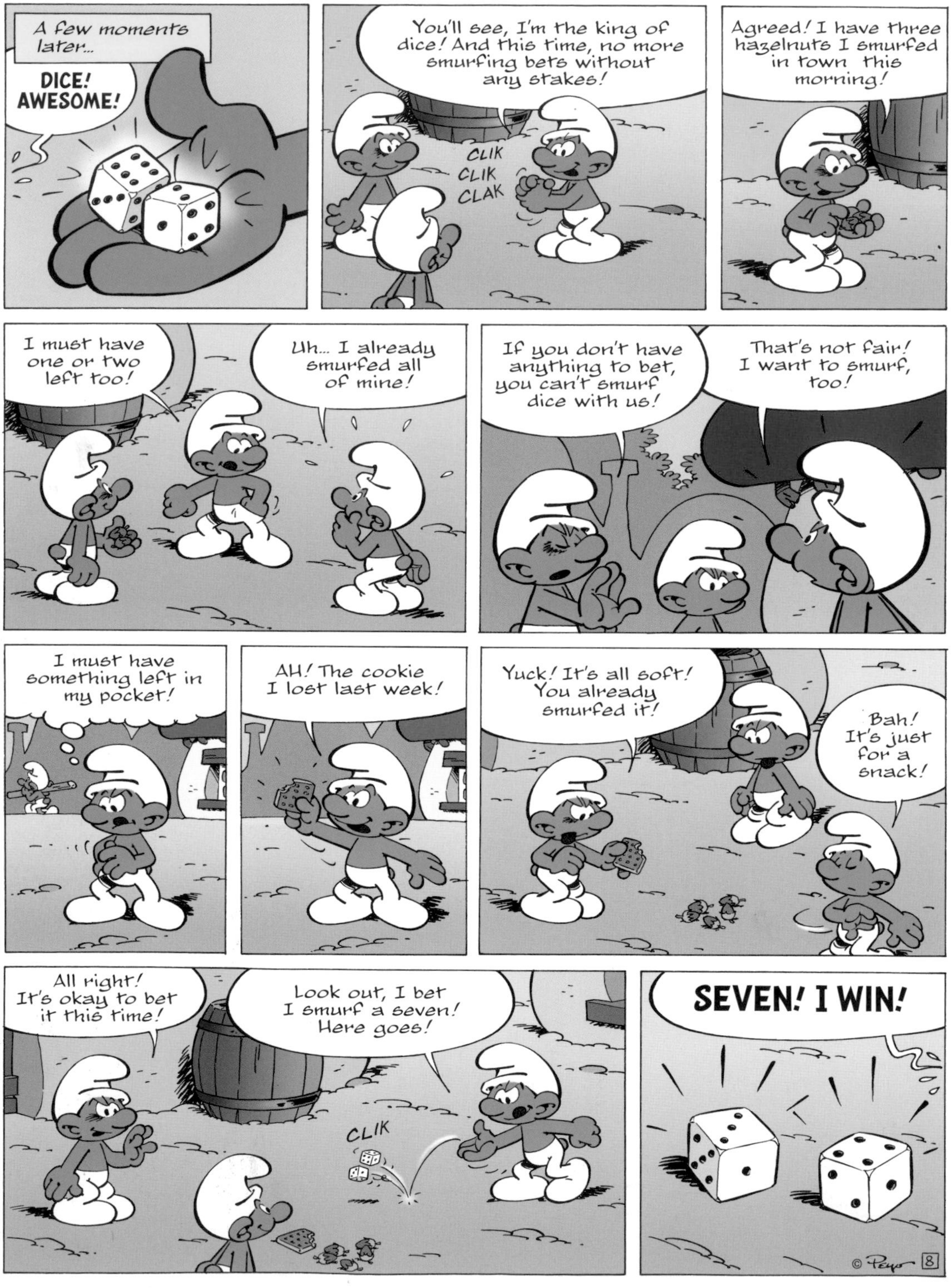
A few moments later...
DICE! AWESOME!
You'll see, I'm the king of dice! And this time, no more smurfing bets without any stakes!
CLIK CLIK CLAK
Agreed! I have three hazelnuts I smurfed in town this morning!
I must have one or two left too!
Uh... I already smurfed all of mine!
If you don't have anything to bet, you can't smurf dice with us!
That's not fair! I want to smurf, too!
I must have something left in my pocket!
AH! The cookie I lost last week!
Yuck! It's all soft! You already smurfed it!
Bah! It's just for a snack!
All right! It's okay to bet it this time!
Look out, I bet I smurf a seven! Here goes!
CLIK
SEVEN! I WIN!
© Peyo 8

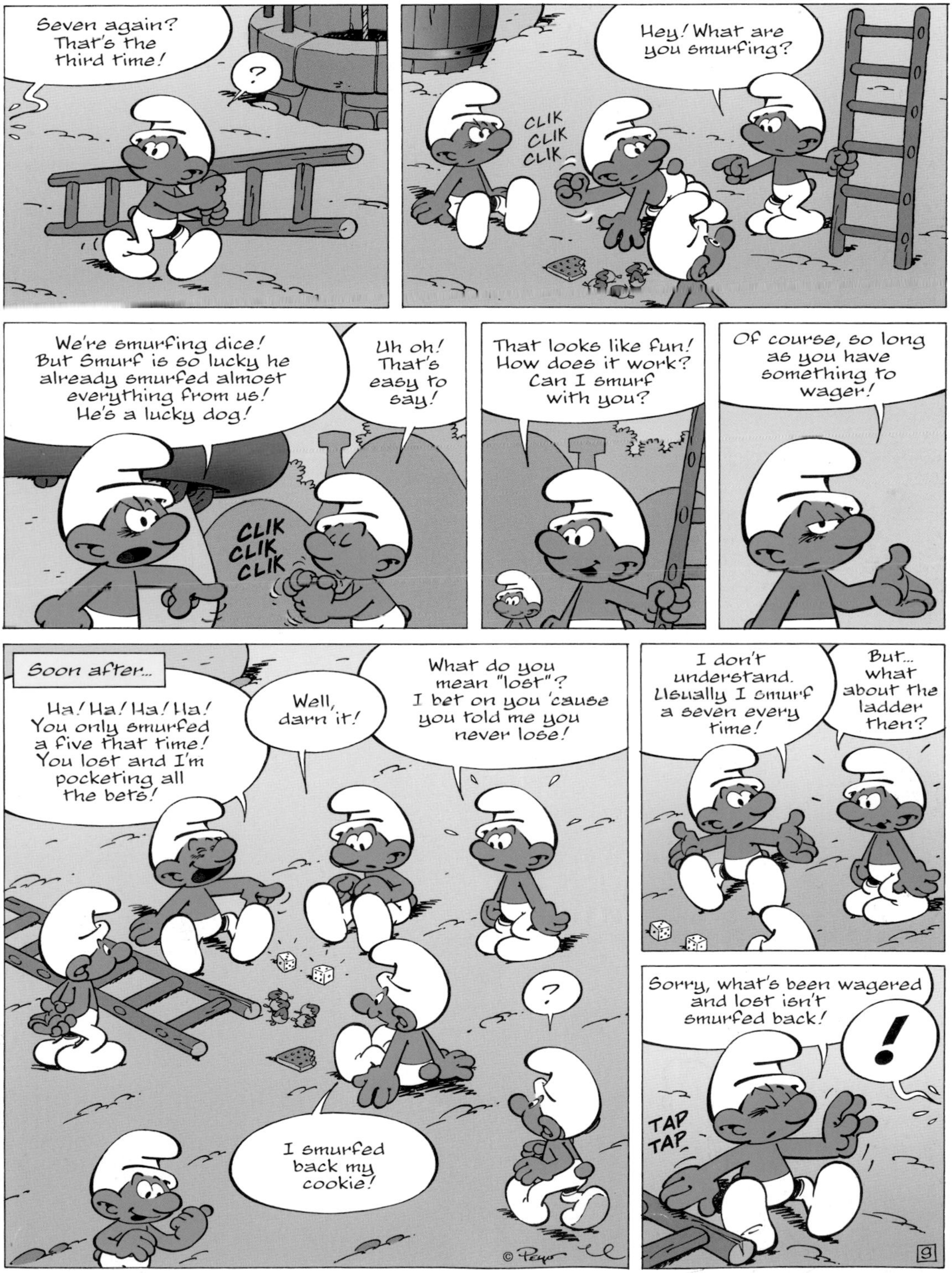
Seven again? That's the third time!
?
Hey! What are you smurfing?
CLIK CLIK CLIK
We're smurfing dice! But Smurf is so lucky he already smurfed almost everything from us! He's a lucky dog!
Uh oh! That's easy to say!
CLIK CLIK CLIK
That looks like fun! How does it work? Can I smurf with you?
Of course, so long as you have something to wager!
Soon after...
Ha! Ha! Ha! Ha! You only smurfed a five that time! You lost and I'm pocketing all the bets!
Well, darn it!
What do you mean "lost"? I bet on you 'cause you told me you never lose!
?
I smurfed back my cookie!
© Peyo
I don't understand. Usually I smurf a seven every time!
But... what about the ladder then?
Sorry, what's been wagered and lost isn't smurfed back!
!
TAP TAP
9

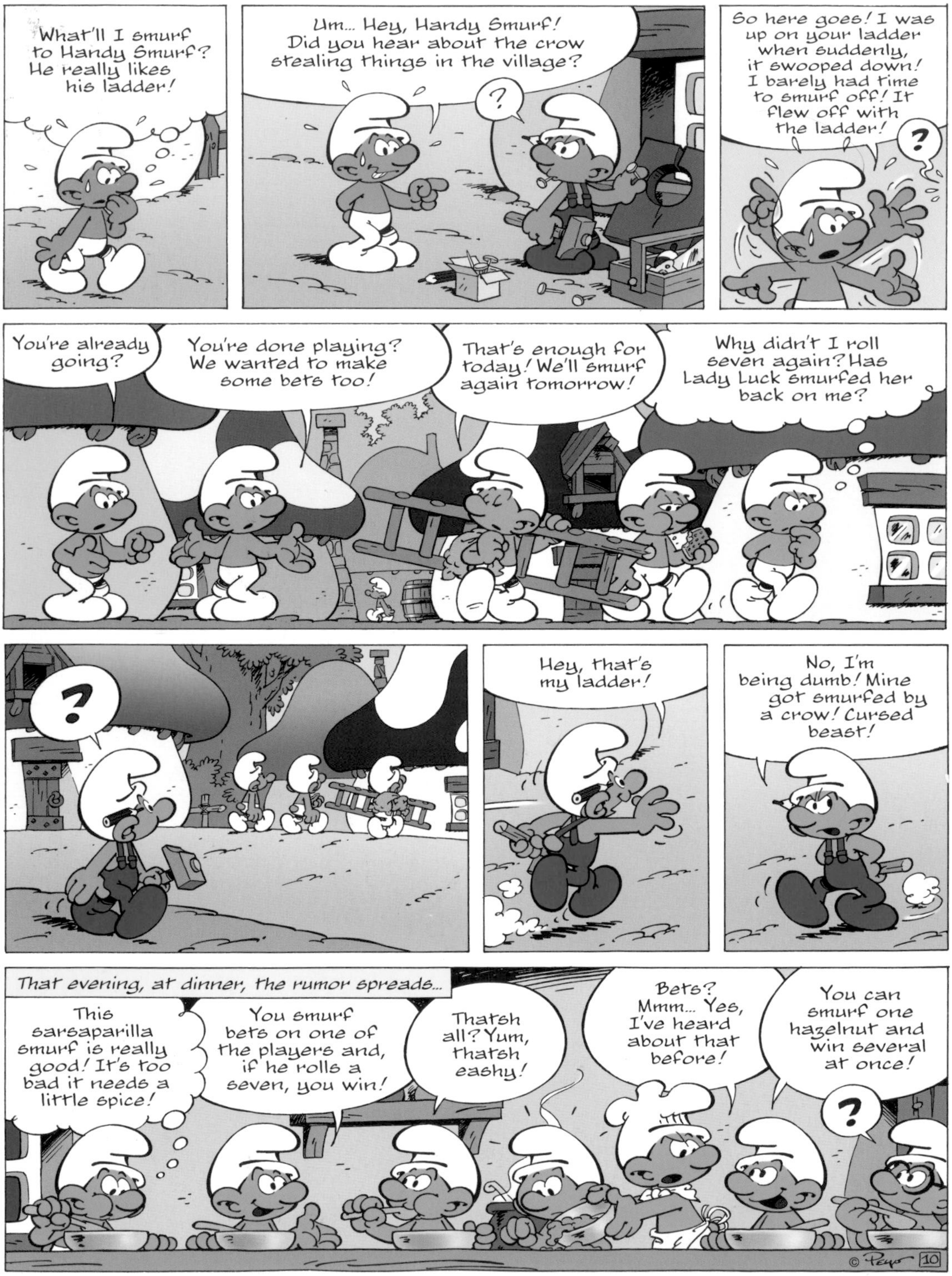
What'll I smurf to Handy Smurf? He really likes his ladder!
Um... Hey, Handy Smurf! Did you hear about the crow stealing things in the village?
?
So here goes! I was up on your ladder when suddenly, it swooped down! I barely had time to smurf off! It flew off with the ladder!
?
You're already going?
You're done playing? We wanted to make some bets too!
That's enough for today! We'll smurf again tomorrow!
Why didn't I roll seven again? Has Lady Luck smurfed her back on me?
?
Hey, that's my ladder!
No, I'm being dumb! Mine got smurfed by a crow! Cursed beast!
That evening, at dinner, the rumor spreads...
This sarsaparilla smurf is really good! It's too bad it needs a little spice!
You smurf bets on one of the players and, if he rolls a seven, you win!
Thatsh all? Yum, thatsh eashy!
Bets? Mmm... Yes, I've heard about that before!
You can smurf one hazelnut and win several at once!
?
© Peyo
10

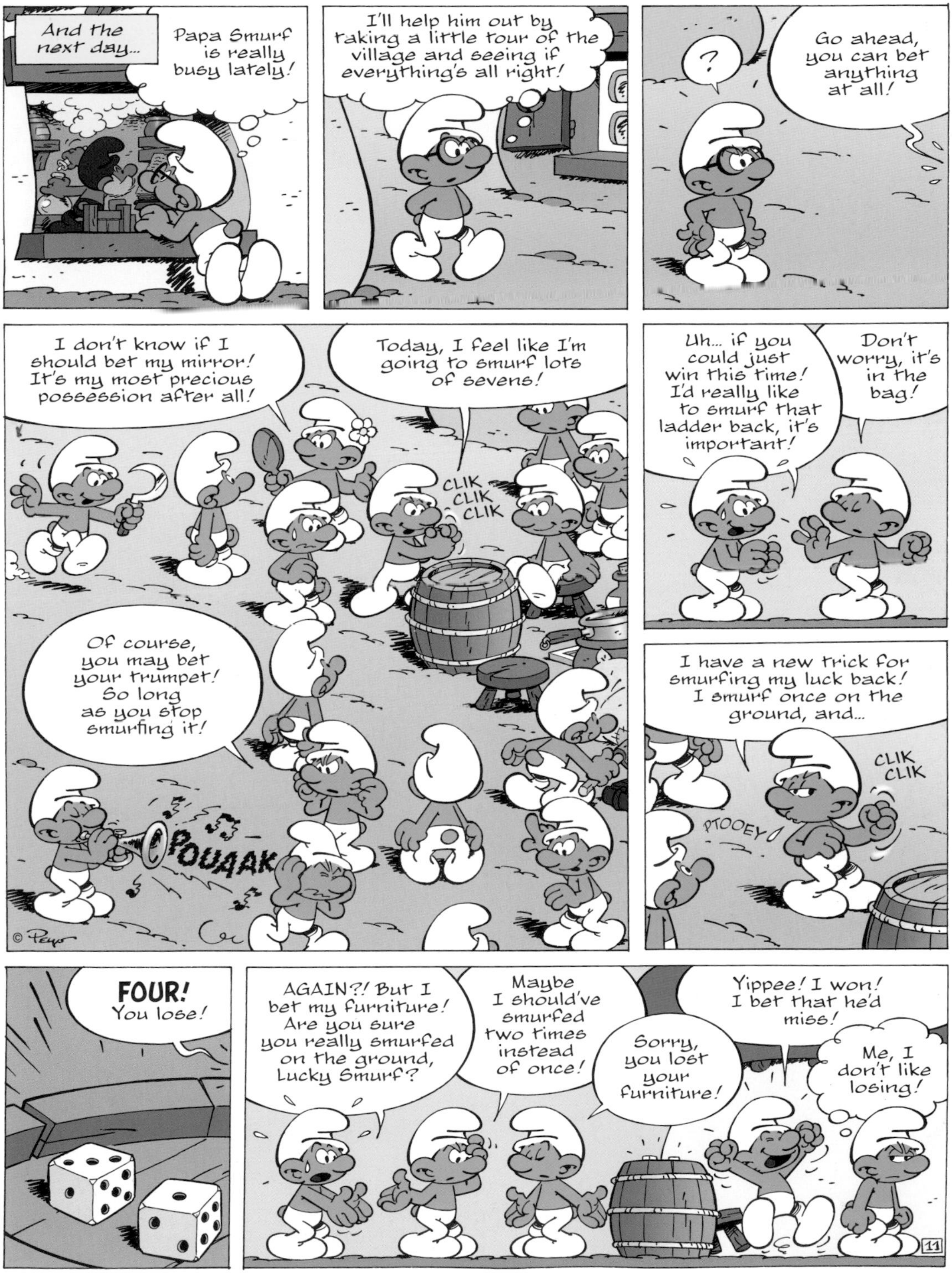
And the next day...
Papa Smurf is really busy lately!
I'll help him out by taking a little tour of the village and seeing if everything's all right!
?
Go ahead, you can bet anything at all!
I don't know if I should bet my mirror! It's my most precious possession after all!
Today, I feel like I'm going to smurf lots of sevens!
CLIK CLIK CLIK
Of course, you may bet your trumpet! So long as you stop smurfing it!
POUAAK
© Peyo
Uh... if you could just win this time! I'd really like to smurf that ladder back, it's important!
Don't worry, it's in the bag!
I have a new trick for smurfing my luck back! I smurf once on the ground, and...
CLIK CLIK
PTOOEY
FOUR! You lose!
AGAIN?! But I bet my furniture! Are you sure you really smurfed on the ground, Lucky Smurf?
Maybe I should've smurfed two times instead of once!
Sorry, you lost your furniture!
Yippee! I won! I bet that he'd miss!
Me, I don't like losing!
11

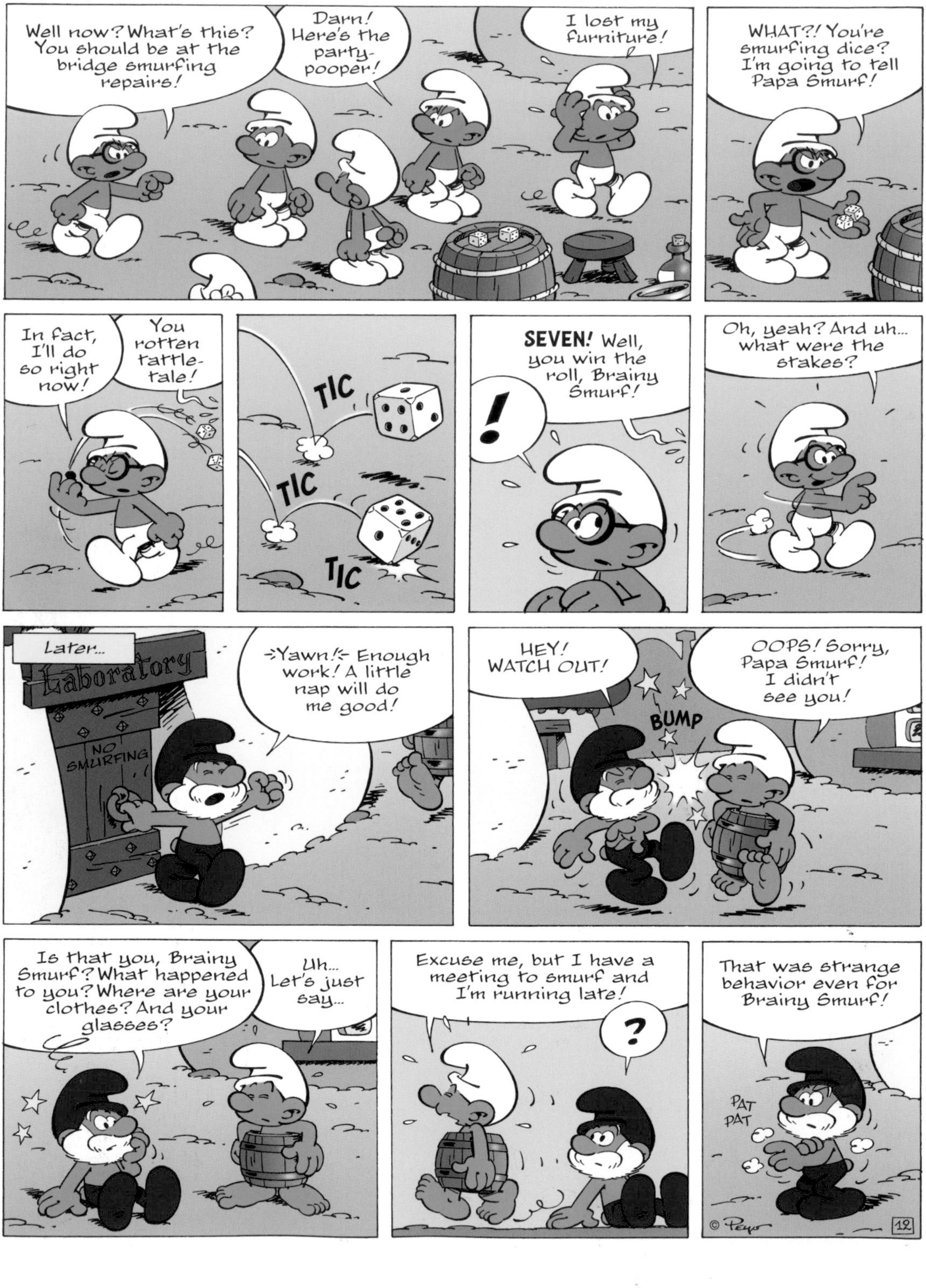
Well now? What's this? You should be at the bridge smurfing repairs!
Darn! Here's the party-pooper!
I lost my furniture!
WHAT?! You're smurfing dice? I'm going to tell Papa Smurf!
In fact, I'll do so right now!
You rotten tattle-tale!
TIC
TIC
TIC
!
SEVEN! Well, you win the roll, Brainy Smurf!
Oh, yeah? And uh... what were the stakes?
Later...
Laboratory
NO SMURFING
-Yawn!- Enough work! A little nap will do me good!
HEY! WATCH OUT!
BUMP
OOPS! Sorry, Papa Smurf! I didn't see you!
Is that you, Brainy Smurf? What happened to you? Where are your clothes? And your glasses?
Uh... Let's just say...
Excuse me, but I have a meeting to smurf and I'm running late!
?
That was strange behavior even for Brainy Smurf!
PAT PAT
© Peyo
12

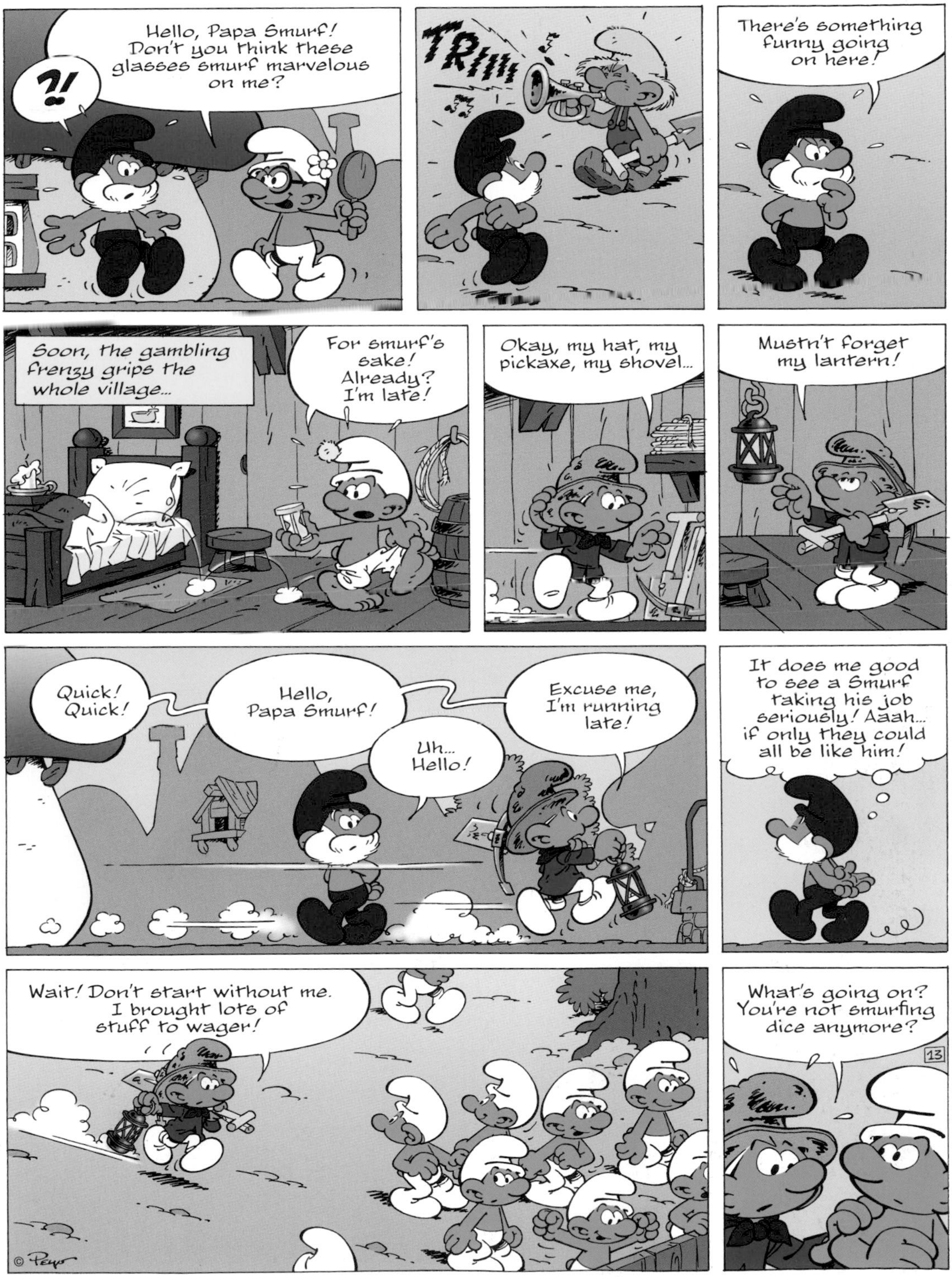

?!
Hello, Papa Smurf! Don't you think these glasses smurf marvelous on me?
TRIIII
There's something funny going on here!
Soon, the gambling frenzy grips the whole village...
For smurf's sake! Already? I'm late!
Okay, my hat, my pickaxe, my shovel...
Mustn't forget my lantern!
Quick! Quick!
Hello, Papa Smurf!
Uh... Hello!
Excuse me, I'm running late!
It does me good to see a Smurf taking his job seriously! Aaah... if only they could all be like him!
Wait! Don't start without me. I brought lots of stuff to wager!
© Peyo
What's going on? You're not smurfing dice anymore?
13

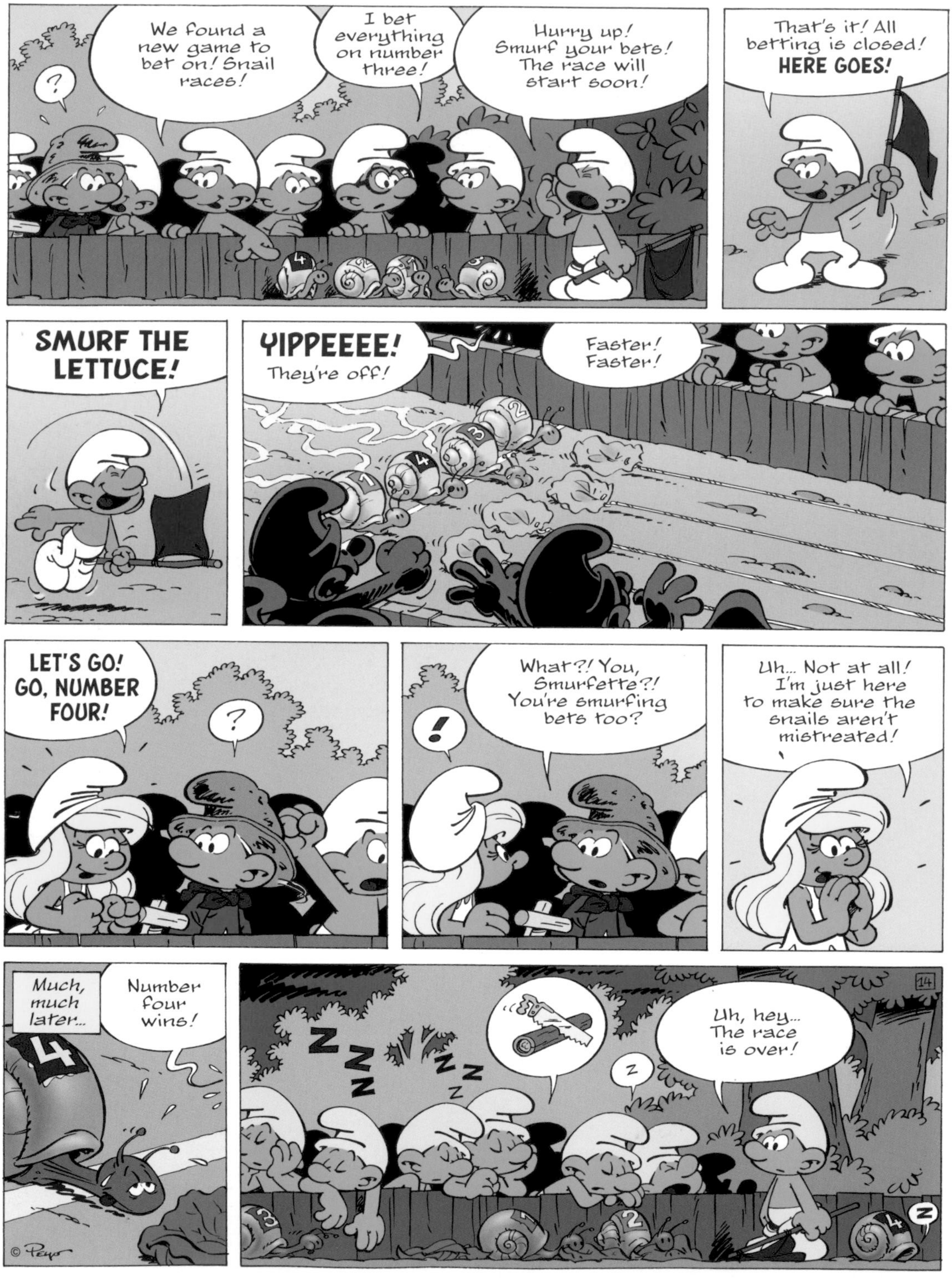

We found a new game to bet on! Snail races!
I bet everything on number three!
Hurry up! Smurf your bets! The race will start soon!
That's it! All betting is closed! **HERE GOES!**
**SMURF THE LETTUCE!**
**YIPPEEEE!** They're off!
Faster! Faster!
**LET'S GO! GO, NUMBER FOUR!**
What?! You, Smurfette?! You're smurfing bets too?
Uh... Not at all! I'm just here to make sure the snails aren't mistreated!
Much, much later...
Number four wins!
Uh, hey... The race is over!
© Peyo

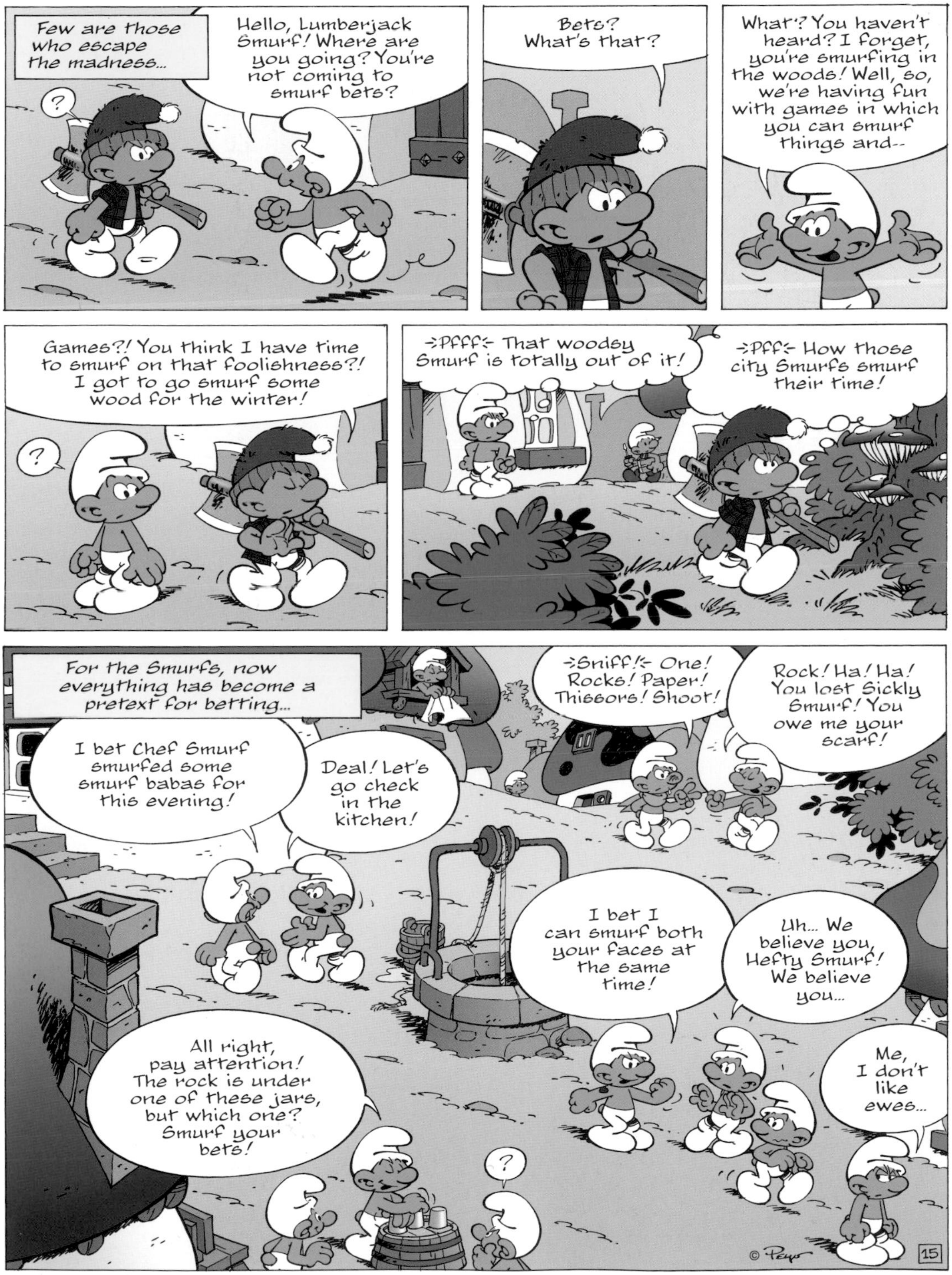
Few are those who escape the madness...
Hello, Lumberjack Smurf! Where are you going? You're not coming to smurf bets?
?
Bets? What's that?
What? You haven't heard? I forget, you're smurfing in the woods! Well, so, we're having fun with games in which you can smurf things and--
Games?! You think I have time to smurf on that foolishness?! I got to go smurf some wood for the winter!
?
=Pfff= That woodsy Smurf is totally out of it!
=Pff= How those city Smurfs smurf their time!
For the Smurfs, now everything has become a pretext for betting...
=Sniff!= One! Rocks! Paper! Thissors! Shoot!
Rock! Ha! Ha! You lost Sickly Smurf! You owe me your scarf!
I bet Chef Smurf smurfed some smurf babas for this evening!
Deal! Let's go check in the kitchen!
I bet I can smurf both your faces at the same time!
Uh... We believe you, Hefty Smurf! We believe you...
All right, pay attention! The rock is under one of these jars, but which one? Smurf your bets!
?
Me, I don't like ewes...
© Peyo
15

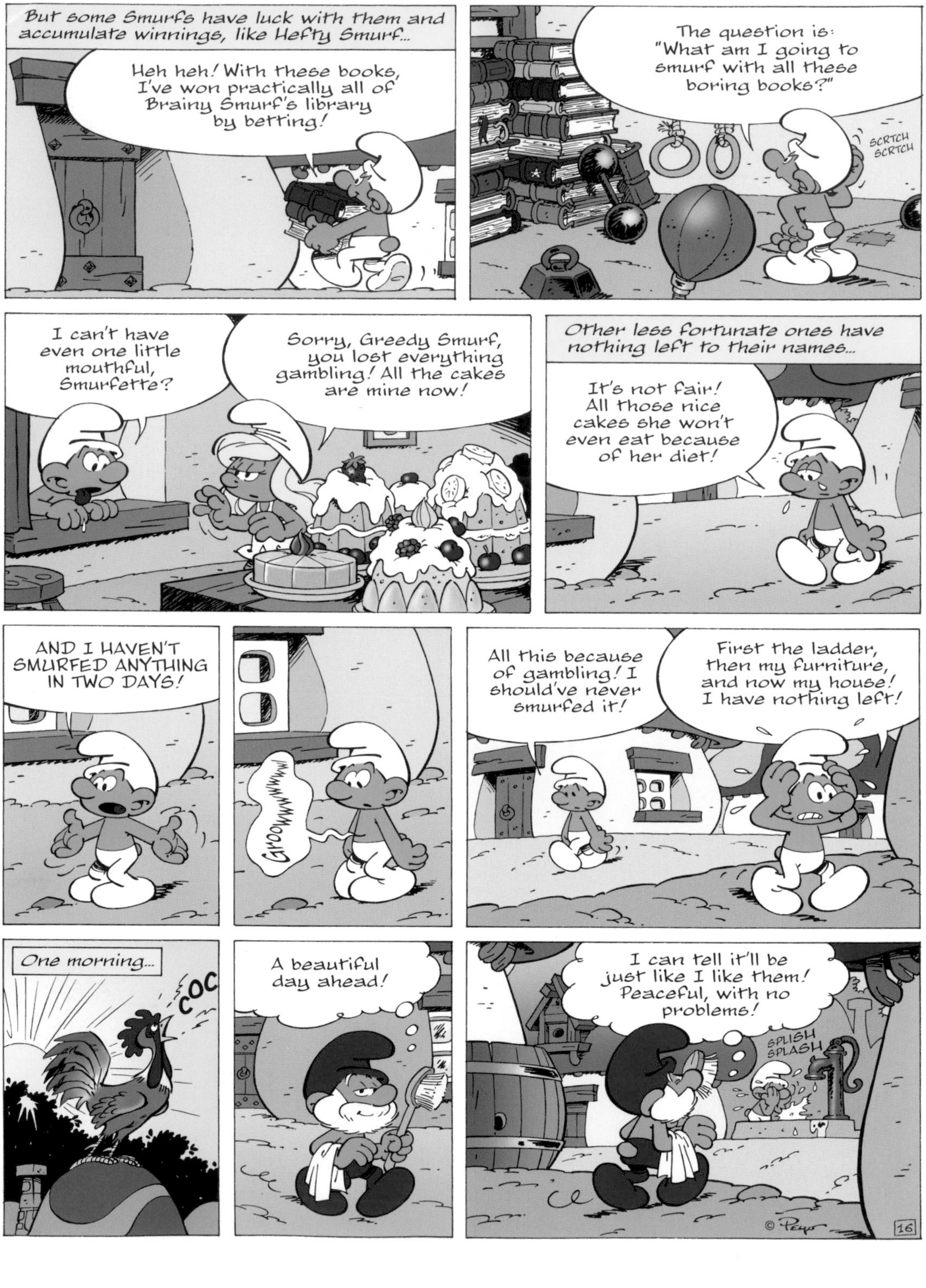

But some Smurfs have luck with them and accumulate winnings, like Hefty Smurf...
Heh heh! With these books, I've won practically all of Brainy Smurf's library by betting!
The question is: "What am I going to smurf with all these boring books?"
SCRTCH SCRTCH
I can't have even one little mouthful, Smurfette?
Sorry, Greedy Smurf, you lost everything gambling! All the cakes are mine now!
Other less fortunate ones have nothing left to their names...
It's not fair! All those nice cakes she won't even eat because of her diet!
AND I HAVEN'T SMURFED ANYTHING IN TWO DAYS!
GROOWWWWWWWWWL
All this because of gambling! I should've never smurfed it!
First the ladder, then my furniture, and now my house! I have nothing left!
One morning...
COC
A beautiful day ahead!
I can tell it'll be just like I like them! Peaceful, with no problems!
SPLISH SPLASH
© Peyo
16

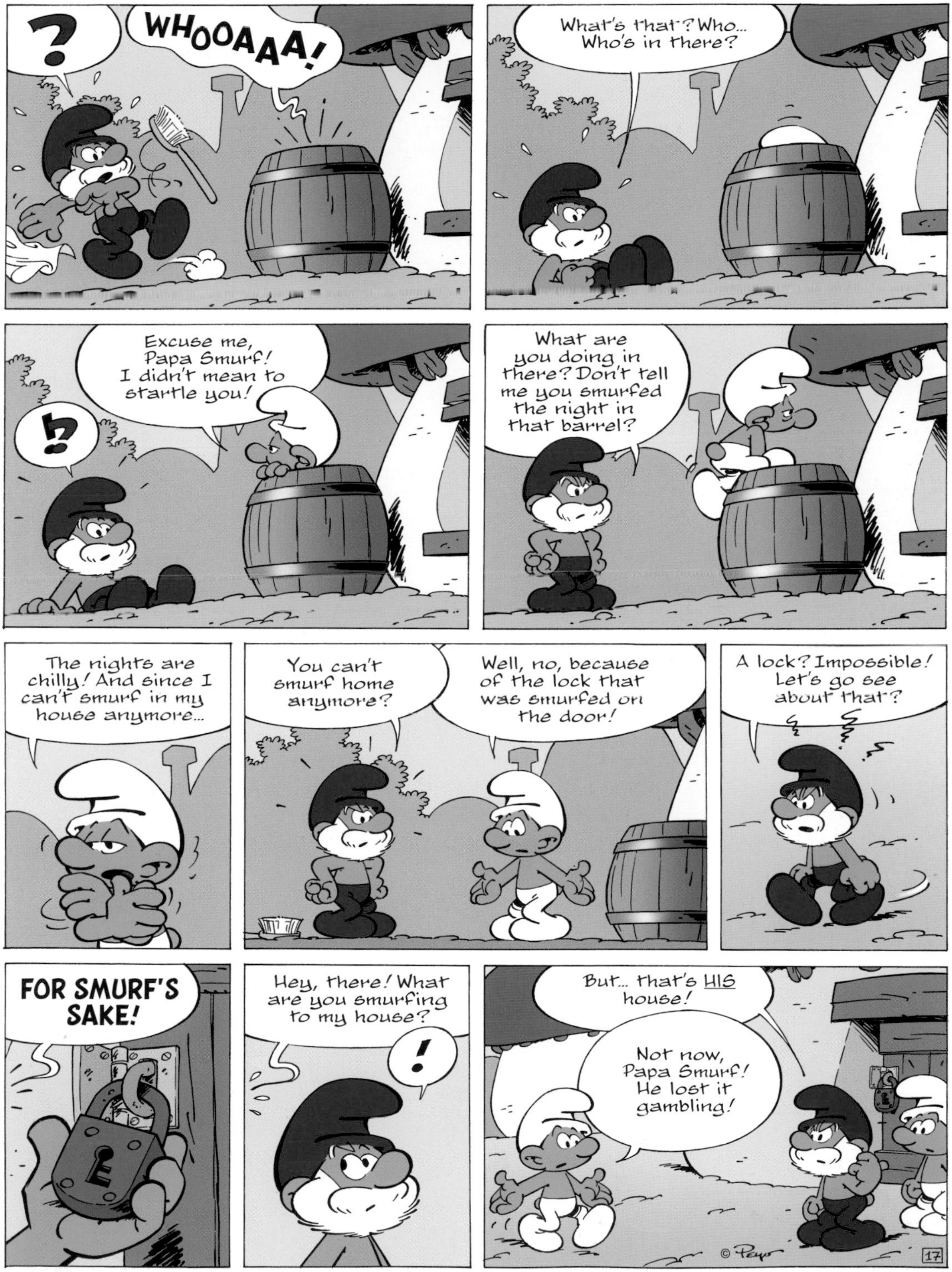
?
WHOOAAA!
What's that? Who... Who's in there?
Excuse me, Papa Smurf! I didn't mean to startle you!
What are you doing in there? Don't tell me you smurfed the night in that barrel?
The nights are chilly! And since I can't smurf in my house anymore...
You can't smurf home anymore?
Well, no, because of the lock that was smurfed on the door!
A lock? Impossible! Let's go see about that?
FOR SMURF'S SAKE!
Hey, there! What are you smurfing to my house?
!
But... that's HIS house!
Not now, Papa Smurf! He lost it gambling!
© Peyo
17

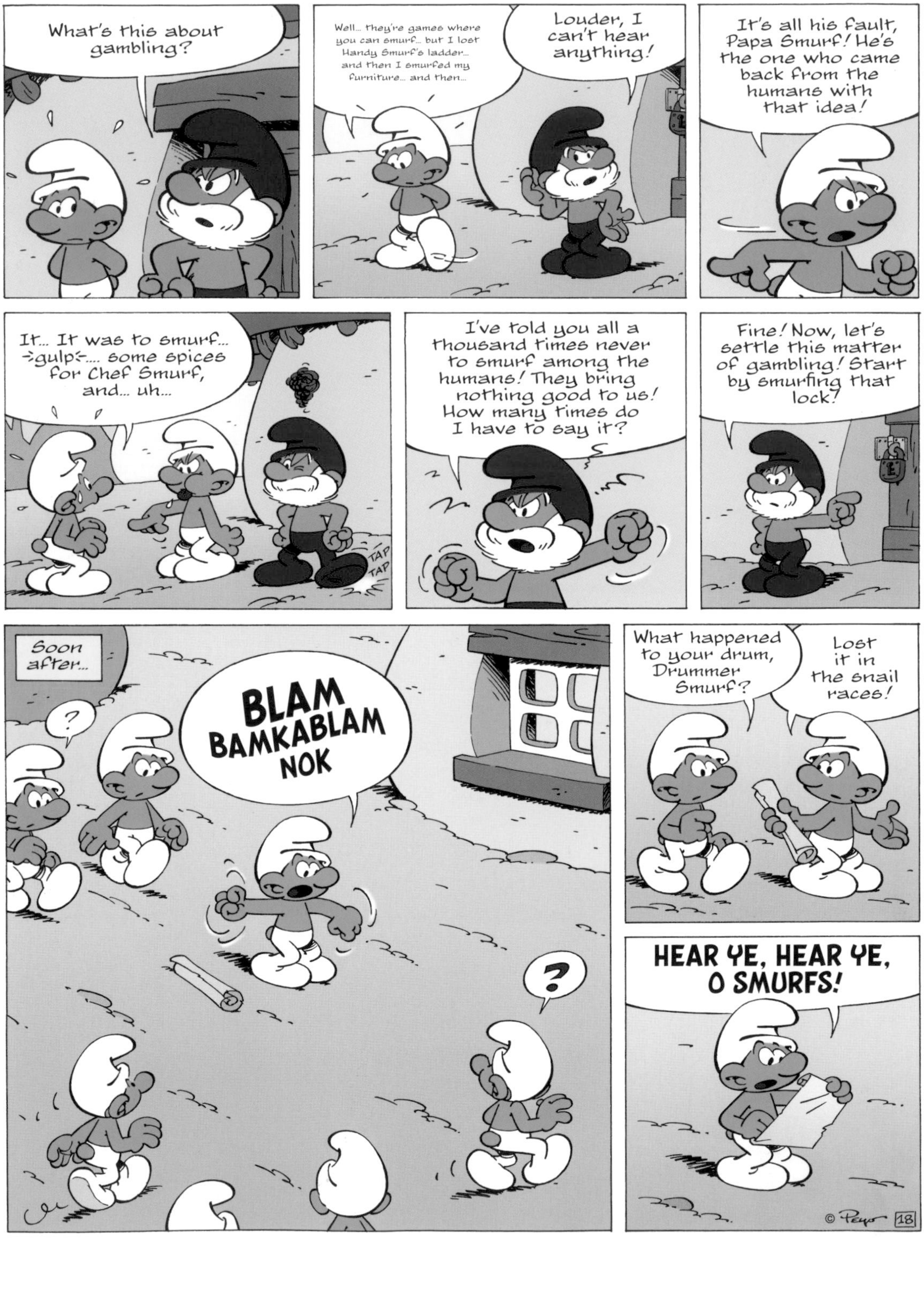
What's this about gambling?
Well... they're games where you can smurf... but I lost Handy Smurf's ladder... and then I smurfed my furniture... and then...
Louder, I can't hear anything!
It's all his fault, Papa Smurf! He's the one who came back from the humans with that idea!
It... It was to smurf... ⇒gulp⇐... some spices for Chef Smurf, and... uh...
TAP TAP
I've told you all a thousand times never to smurf among the humans! They bring nothing good to us! How many times do I have to say it?
Fine! Now, let's settle this matter of gambling! Start by smurfing that lock!
Soon after...
?
BLAM BAMKABLAM NOK
?
What happened to your drum, Drummer Smurf?
Lost it in the snail races!
HEAR YE, HEAR YE, O SMURFS!
© Peyo
18

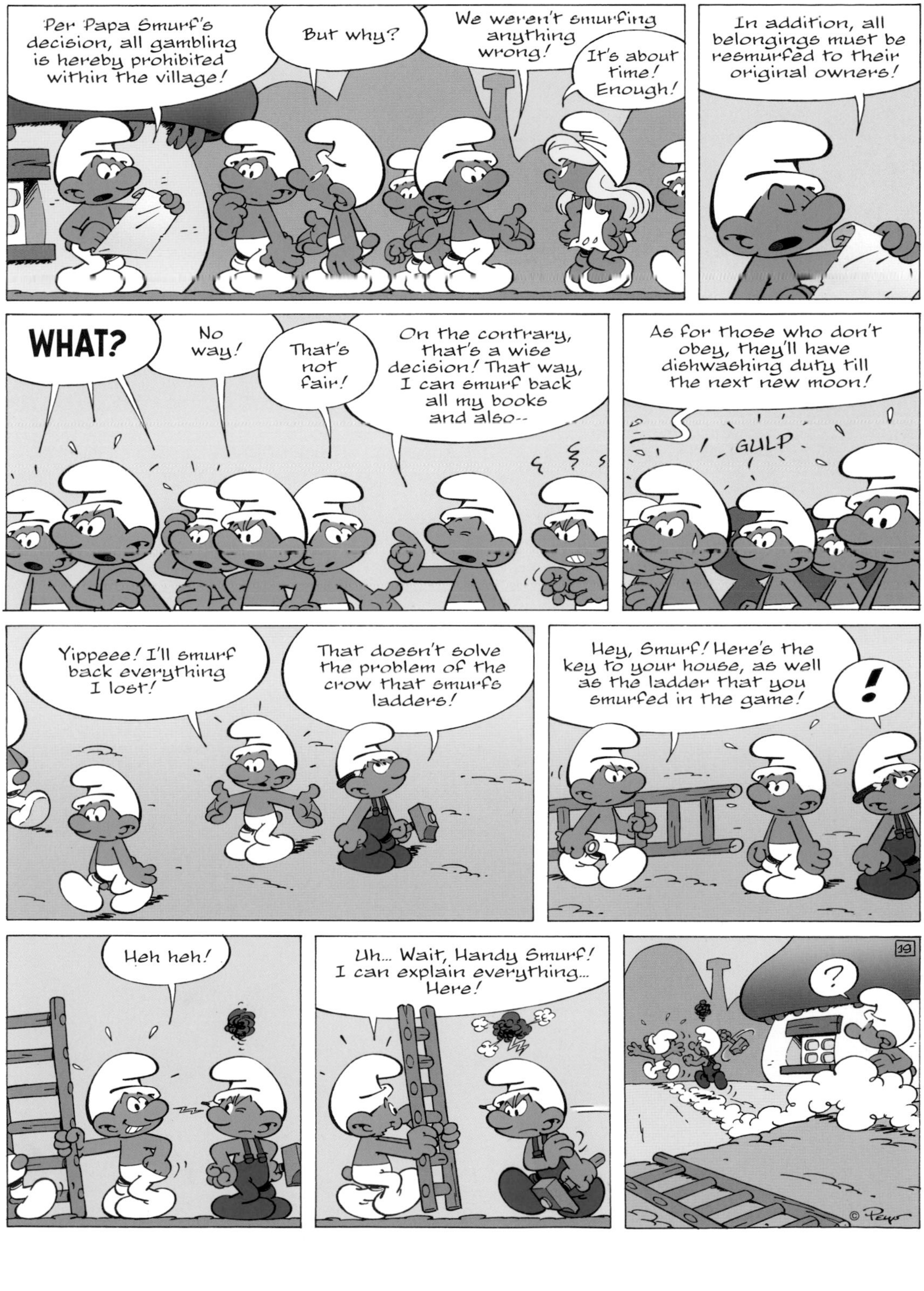
Per Papa Smurf's decision, all gambling is hereby prohibited within the village!
But why?
We weren't smurfing anything wrong!
It's about time! Enough!
In addition, all belongings must be resmurfed to their original owners!
WHAT?
No way!
That's not fair!
On the contrary, that's a wise decision! That way, I can smurf back all my books and also--
As for those who don't obey, they'll have dishwashing duty till the next new moon!
GULP
Yippeee! I'll smurf back everything I lost!
That doesn't solve the problem of the crow that smurfs ladders!
Hey, Smurf! Here's the key to your house, as well as the ladder that you smurfed in the game!
!
Heh heh!
Uh... Wait, Handy Smurf! I can explain everything... Here!
19
?
© Peyo

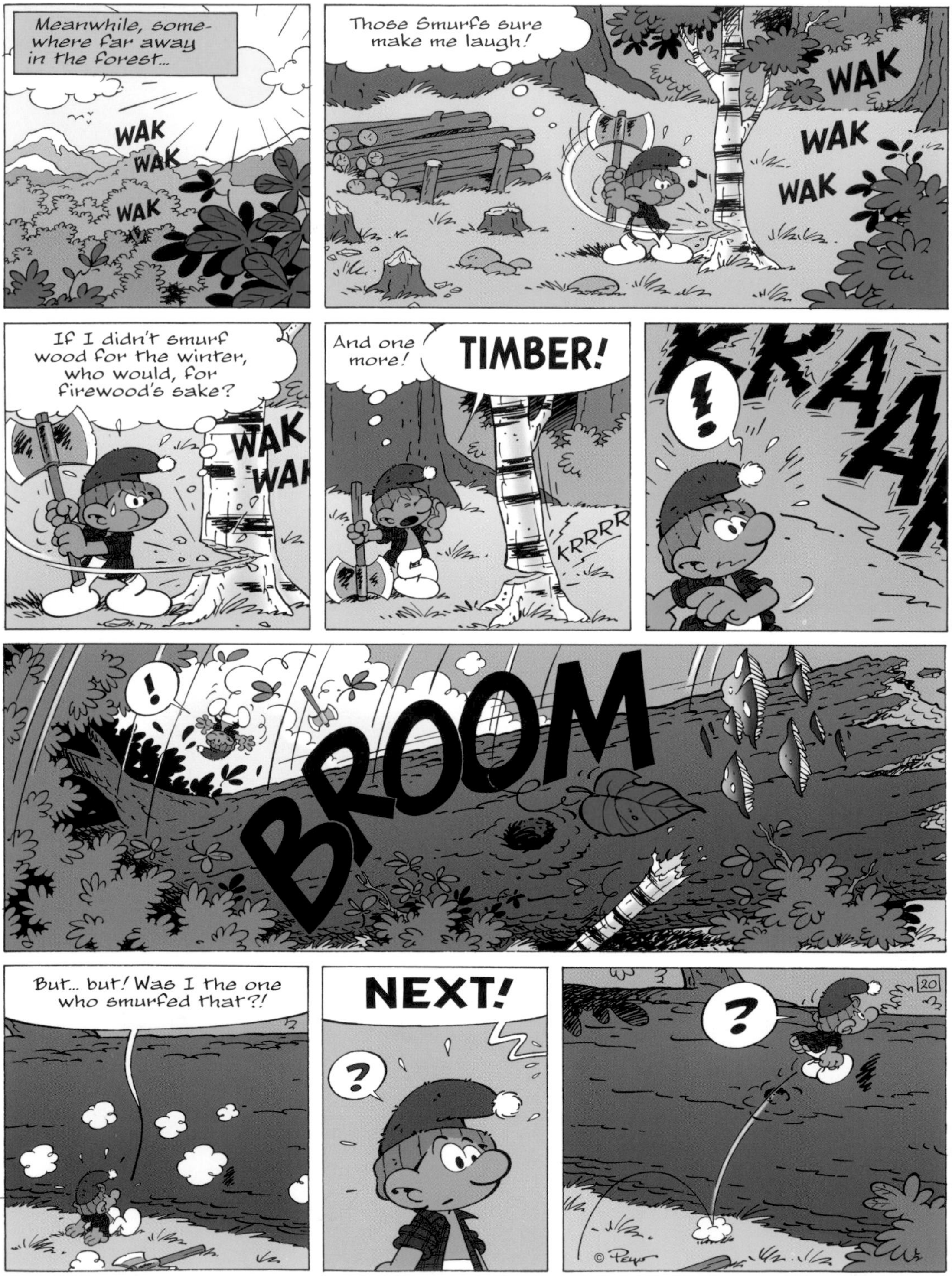

Meanwhile, somewhere far away in the forest...
WAK
WAK
WAK
Those Smurfs sure make me laugh!
WAK
WAK
WAK
If I didn't smurf wood for the winter, who would, for firewood's sake?
WAK
And one more!
TIMBER!
KRRRR
!
!
BROOM
But... but! Was I the one who smurfed that?!
NEXT!
?
?
20
© Peyo

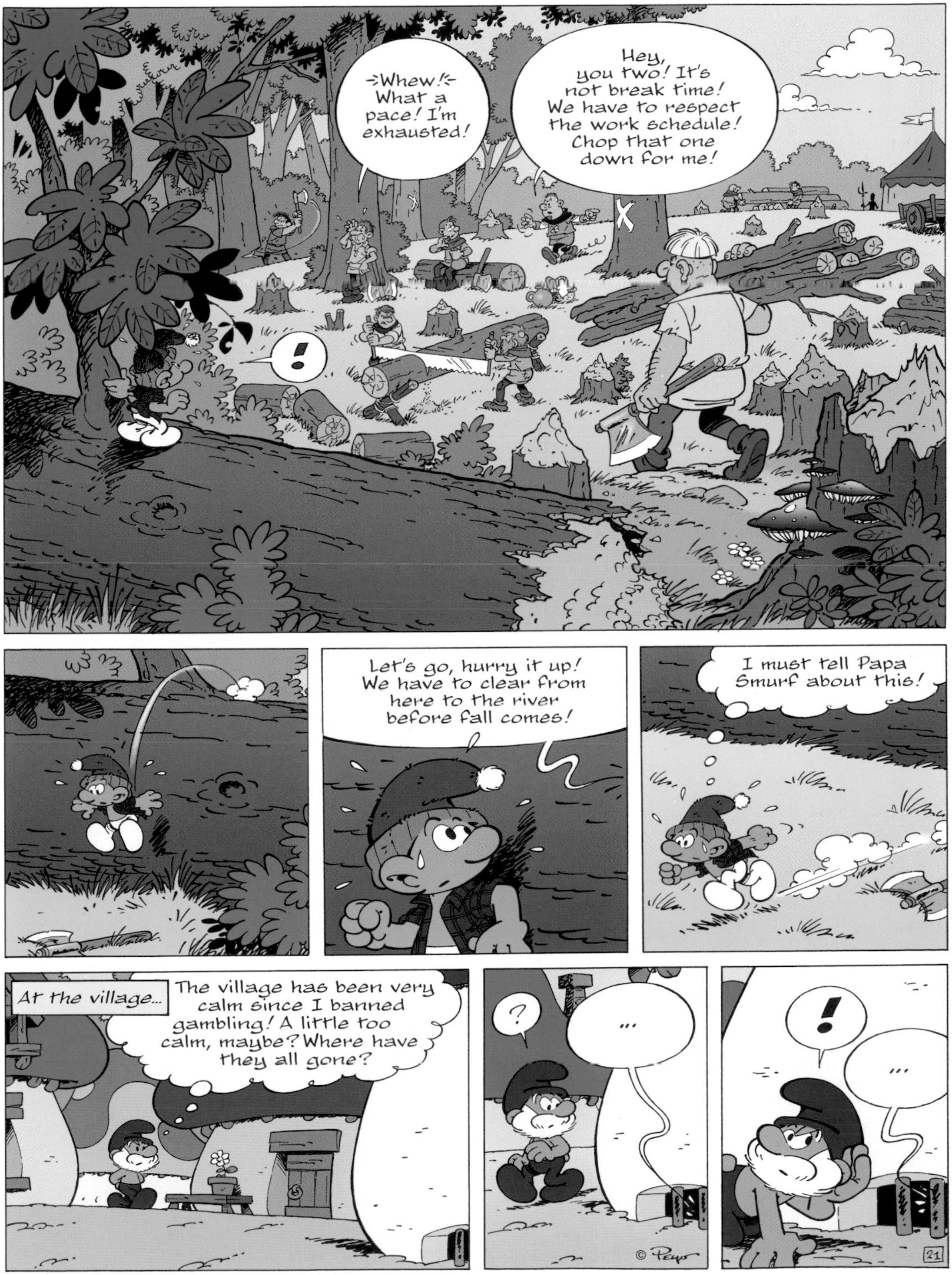

Whew! What a pace! I'm exhausted!
Hey, you two! It's not break time! We have to respect the work schedule! Chop that one down for me!
!
Let's go, hurry it up! We have to clear from here to the river before fall comes!
I must tell Papa Smurf about this!
At the village...
The village has been very calm since I banned gambling! A little too calm, maybe? Where have they all gone?
?
...
!
...
© Peyo
21

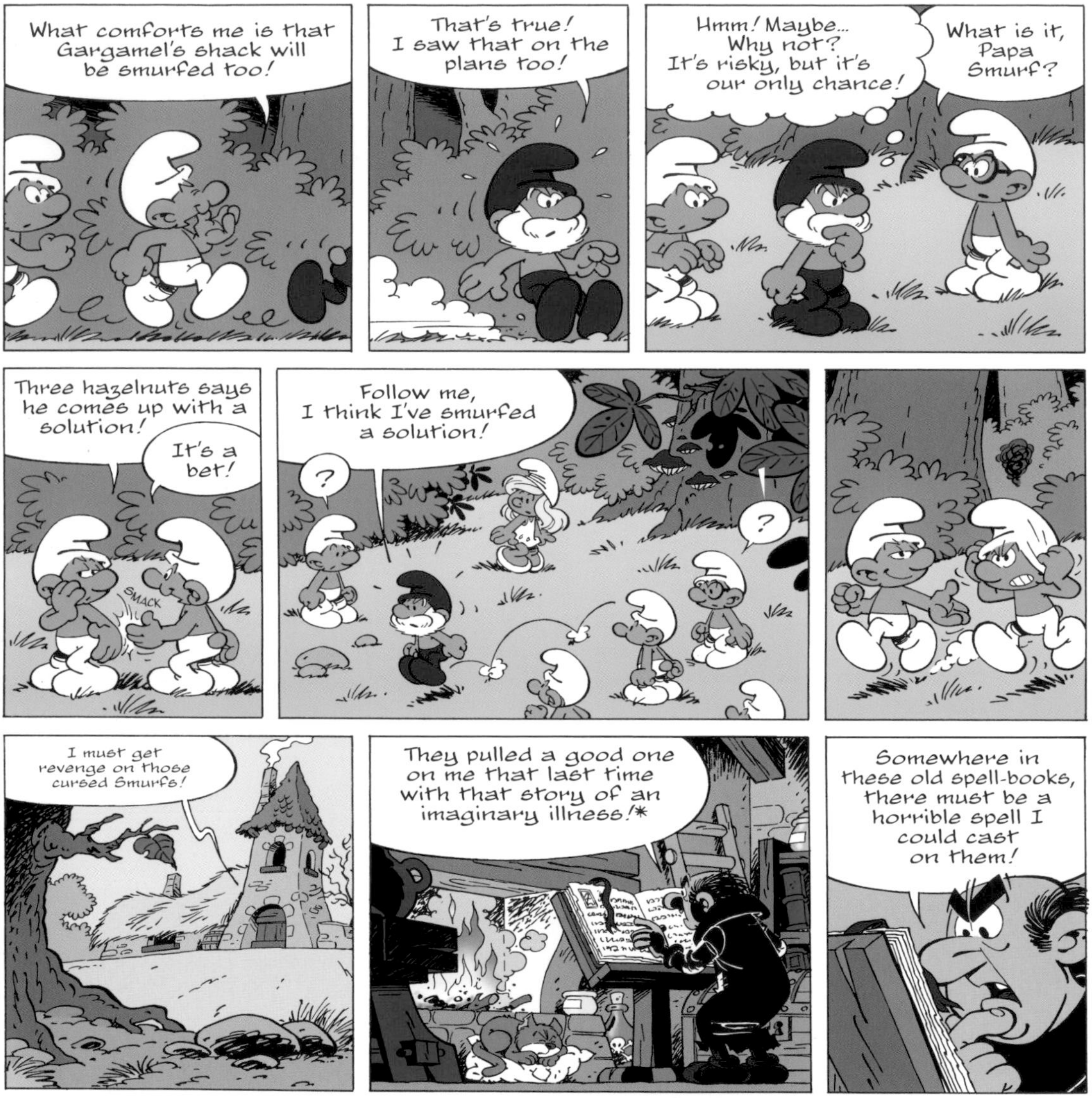
What comforts me is that Gargamel's shack will be smurfed too!
That's true! I saw that on the plans too!
Hmm! Maybe... Why not? It's risky, but it's our only chance!
What is it, Papa Smurf?
Three hazelnuts says he comes up with a solution!
It's a bet!
SMACK
Follow me, I think I've smurfed a solution!
?
!
?
I must get revenge on those cursed Smurfs!
They pulled a good one on me that last time with that story of an imaginary illness!*
Somewhere in these old spell-books, there must be a horrible spell I could cast on them!
?
NOK NOK
Who could that be?
THE SMURFS!
26
© Peyo

* See: THE SMURFS #24 "The Smurf Reporter."

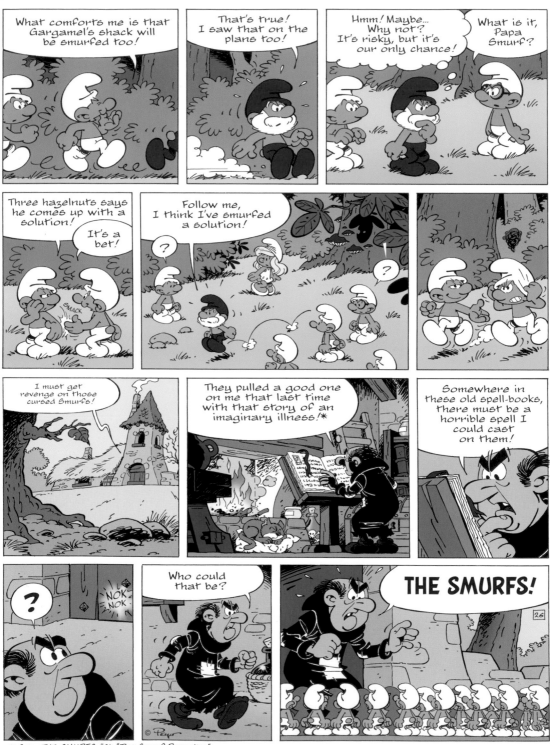

29

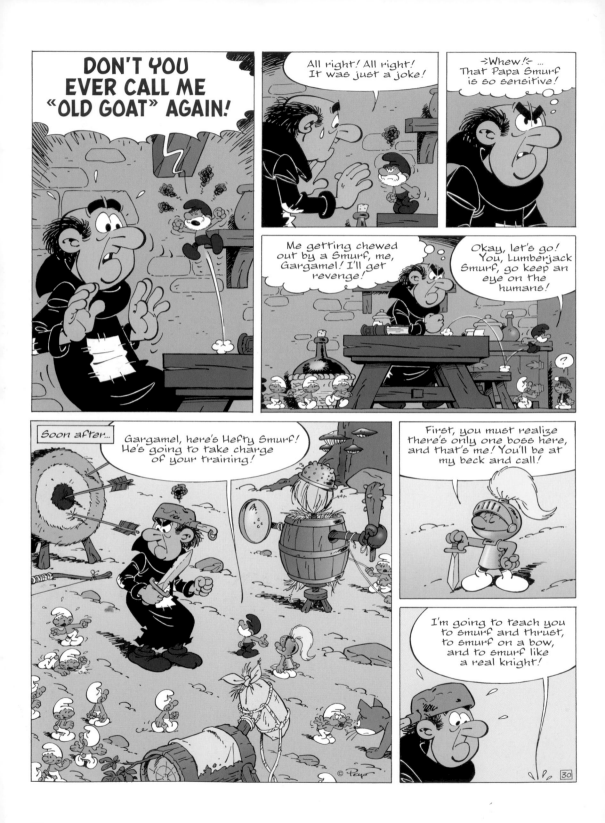

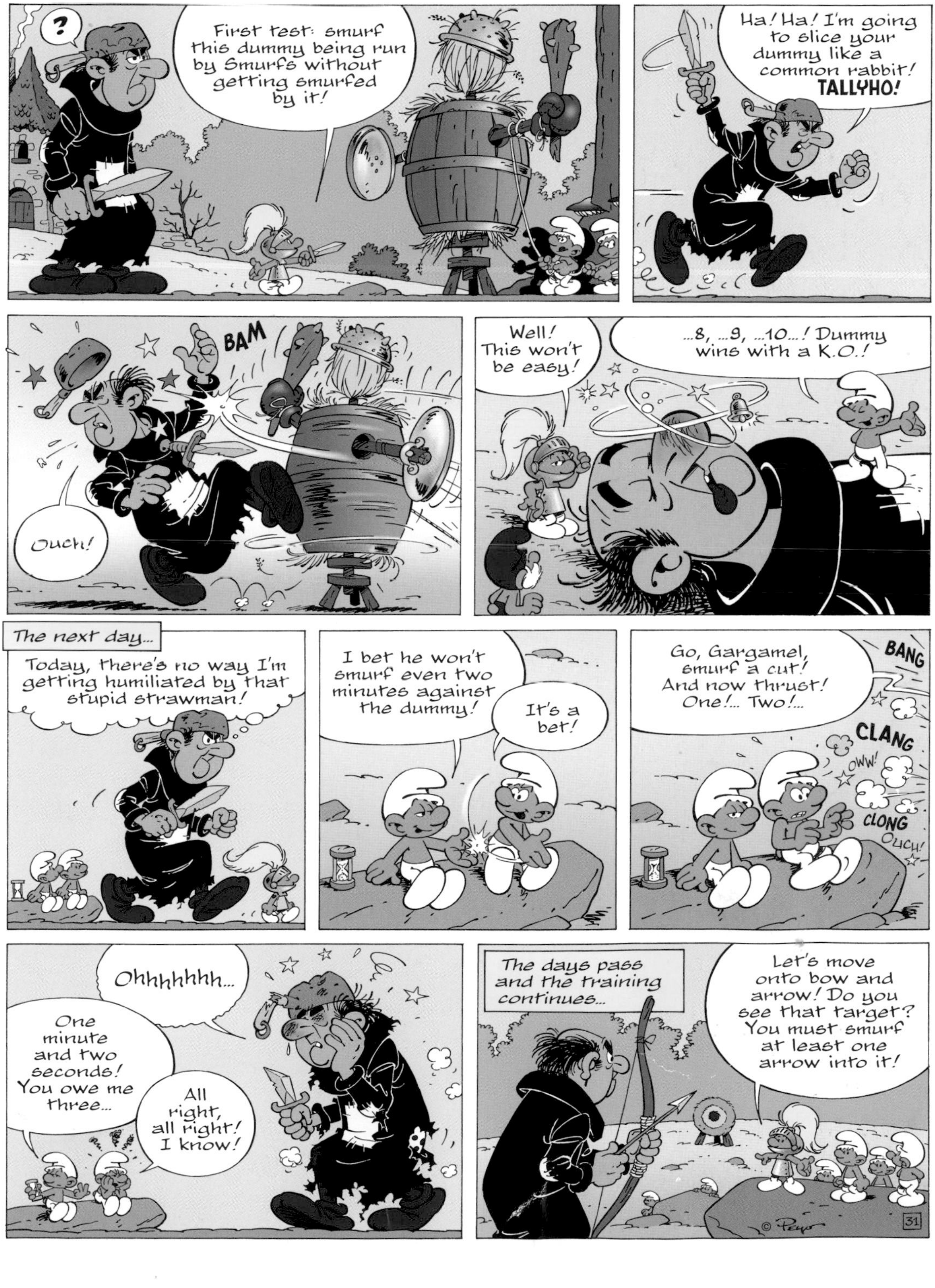
?
First test: smurf this dummy being run by Smurfs without getting smurfed by it!
Ha! Ha! I'm going to slice your dummy like a common rabbit! TALLYHO!
BAM
Ouch!
Well! This won't be easy!
...8, ...9, ...10...! Dummy wins with a K.O.!
The next day...
Today, there's no way I'm getting humiliated by that stupid strawman!
I bet he won't smurf even two minutes against the dummy!
It's a bet!
Go, Gargamel, smurf a cut! And now thrust! One!... Two!...
BANG
CLANG
OWW!
CLONG
OUCH!
Ohhhhhhh...
One minute and two seconds! You owe me three...
All right, all right! I know!
The days pass and the training continues...
Let's move onto bow and arrow! Do you see that target? You must smurf at least one arrow into it!
© Peyo
31

34

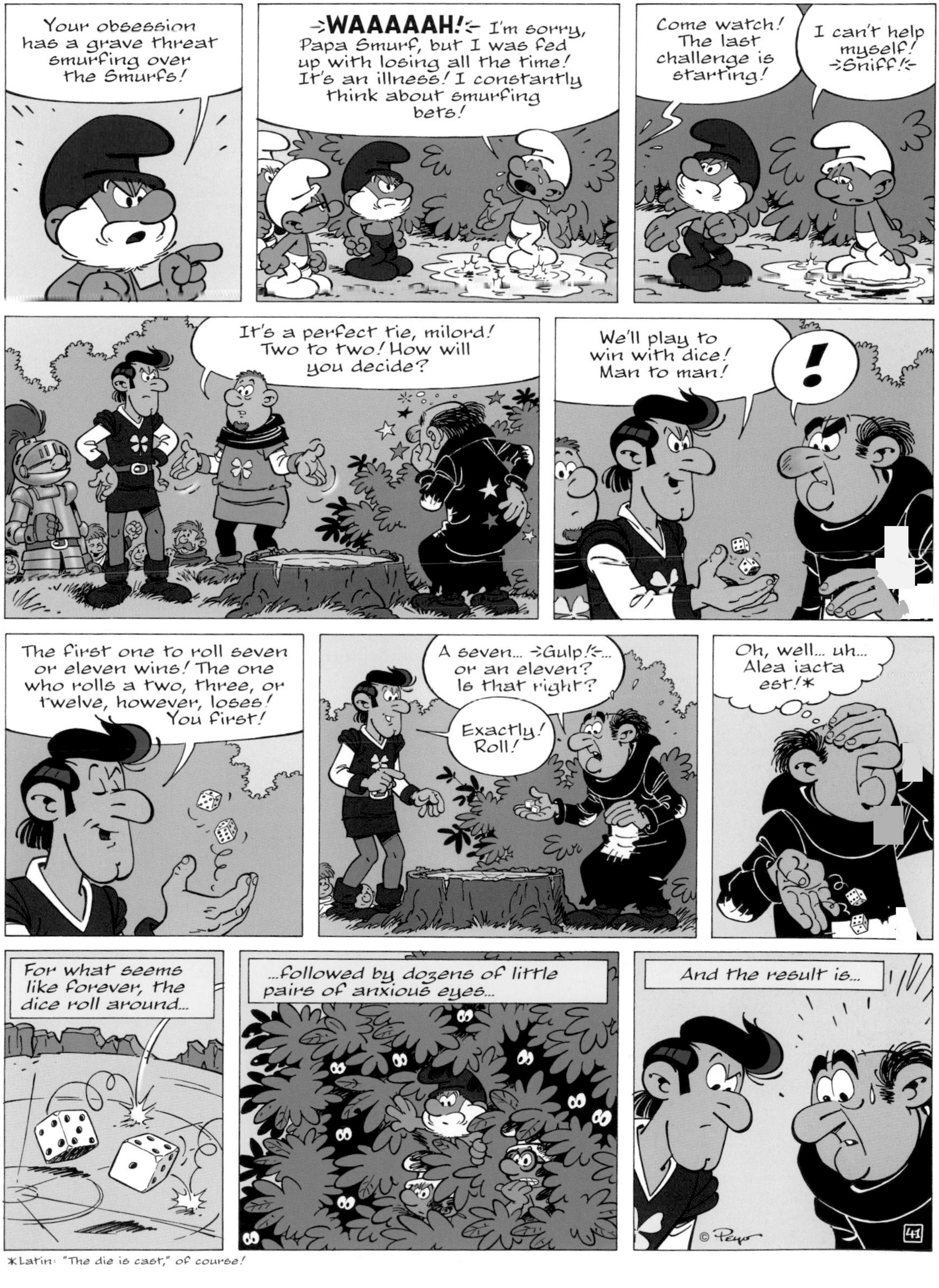

Your obsession has a grave threat smurfing over the Smurfs!
-WAAAAAH!- I'm sorry, Papa Smurf, but I was fed up with losing all the time! It's an illness! I constantly think about smurfing bets!
Come watch! The last challenge is starting!
I can't help myself! -Sniff!-
It's a perfect tie, milord! Two to two! How will you decide?
We'll play to win with dice! Man to man!
!
The first one to roll seven or eleven wins! The one who rolls a two, three, or twelve, however, loses! You first!
A seven... -Gulp!-... or an eleven? Is that right?
Exactly! Roll!
Oh, well... uh... Alea iacta est!*
For what seems like forever, the dice roll around...
...followed by dozens of little pairs of anxious eyes...
And the result is...
© Peyo
41


*Latin: "The die is cast," of course!

45

# WATCH OUT FOR PAPERCUTZ™

If you bet that I was going to start this page by writing, "Welcome to the tournament-wagering twenty-fifth SMURFS graphic novel by Peyo, from Papercutz, those poker-faced people dedicated to publishing great graphic novels for all ages." Then you just won your bet[1]. But can you tell me how you knew? Because if you could've told me what I was going to write, it would've saved me a little time! Oh, and I'm Jim Salicrup, by the way, the lucky scratch card-playing Smurf-in-Chief, with some smurfy reflections on our 25th Smurfversary…

We're all smurfcited that this is our 25th SMURFS graphic novel, not counting all THE SMURFS specials, THE SMURFS AND FRIENDS, THE SMURFS ANTHOLOGY, and all the other SMURFS books (and comicbooks) we've been proudly publishing since 2010. Believe it or not, when we at Papercutz first launched our first two SMURFS graphic novels, we had no idea if the series would sell well enough to allow us to publish any further volumes. We certainly hoped it would, but being a relatively small publisher (about three apples tall) constantly battling for survival against our much bigger competitors, we can never be certain. Let's face it, publishing is like gambling. With every graphic novel Papercutz publishes, we can either win or lose. When we lose, we hope we're able to move on and try publishing other graphic novels that will fare better. If we win, we get to publish more of the graphic novels we love.

Fortunately, our betting on THE SMURFS paid off big-time, but I still remember thinking that those two initial SMURFS graphic novels might've been the only SMURFS graphic novels ever published by Papercutz. Therefore I had to carefully choose the two I most wanted to see published in North America. It was like a Smurf-genie was granting me only two wishes. The first choice was easy: "The Purple Smurfs." While most of THE SMURFS graphic novels had been translated into English at some point, this one never had been[2], despite being adapted into one of the early episodes on the hit, long-running Saturday morning animated TV series. The second choice was tough too: "The Smurfs and the Magic Flute." This

wasn't even technically a SMURFS story, it was an episode of Peyo's *Johan and Peewit* series, but it was the story that first introduced the Smurfs over sixty years ago, How could we not want to publish this one?

Which brings us back to this 25th Papercutz SMURFS graphic novel, and in addition to featuring "The Gambling Smurfs," we're presenting the conclusion to "The Flute Smurfers," the special prequel to "The Smurfs and the Magic Flute." This story was originally created ten years ago, just a year or so before Papercutz started publishing THE SMURFS, to celebrate the fiftieth anniversary of THE SMURFS. We presented it in its entirety in THE SMURFS AND FRIENDS Volume One, but we thought it would be fun to re-present it to both celebrate the sixtieth anniversary of THE SMURFS in THE SMURFS #24 and here to celebrate our twenty-fifth volume of THE SMURFS!

Now if it turns out that you missed "The Smurfs and the Magic Flute," and you want to see what happens next after "The Flute Smurfers," don't worry—you have loads of options. You can either go to your favorite bookstore, library, or on-line (www.comixology.com, for example) and find that story in any one of the following: THE SMURFS #2 "The Smurfs and the Magic Flute," THE SMURFS 3 IN 1 #1, or THE SMURFS ANTHOLOGY Volume One. And if you've already enjoyed that classic tale, be sure to join us for THE SMURFS #26 "Smurf Salad," and don't forget to look for the all-new Smurfs animated series, both coming soon! There's never any reason to be without Smurfs!

Smurf you later *Jim*

[1]Of course, we at Papercutz don't encourage gambling of any kind, but if you do ever gamble, our advice is to never bet more than you can afford to lose.
[2]For the full story, check out Smurfologist Matt. Murray's introduction to "The Purple Smurfs" in THE SMURFS ANTHOLOGY Volume One.

## STAY IN TOUCH!

| | |
|---|---|
| EMAIL: | salicrup@papercutz.com |
| WEB: | papercutz.com |
| TWITTER: | @papercutzgn |
| INSTAGRAM: | @papercutzgn |
| FACEBOOK: | PAPERCUTZGRAPHICNOVELS |
| FANMAIL: | Papercutz, 160 Broadway, Suite 700, East Wing, New York, NY 10038 |

# THE FLUTE SMURFERS Conclusion

## *PREVIOUSLY IN THE SMURFS #24...*

*A stork arrived at the Smurf Village with an important message for Papa Smurf from his friend, the sorcerer Alderic, asking him to create a magic flute. The magic flute would be to cure one of his patients with a "Monotone Melancholy," an illness that humans are especially susceptible to which fills them with apathy to the point that they'll not make the slightest move all day long. The Smurfs create the magic flute and deliver it to him. Alderic explains to Papa Smurf that Emile, a peasant, contracted the illness after carelessly walking through a fairy ring. With the village doctor unable to help Emile, his wife came to Alderic for help. The Smurfs and the sorcerer bring the magic flute to Emile's home, play the flute, and the peasant hops out of bed cured! Little did they know that the village doctor was right outside the house and witnessed Emile's remarkable recovery. The doctor, scheming to get rid of Alderic, decides he must have the magic flute. After Alderic and the Smurfs leave, Papa Smurf realizes he forgot to give Emile an important bit of advice, and rushes back alone to the peasant's home. He's ambushed by the village doctor, who knocks out Papa Smurf and takes the magic flute. The Smurfs decide they must enter the village, to reclaim the flute. They see their chance to hop on a coalman's cart as he's entering the village...*

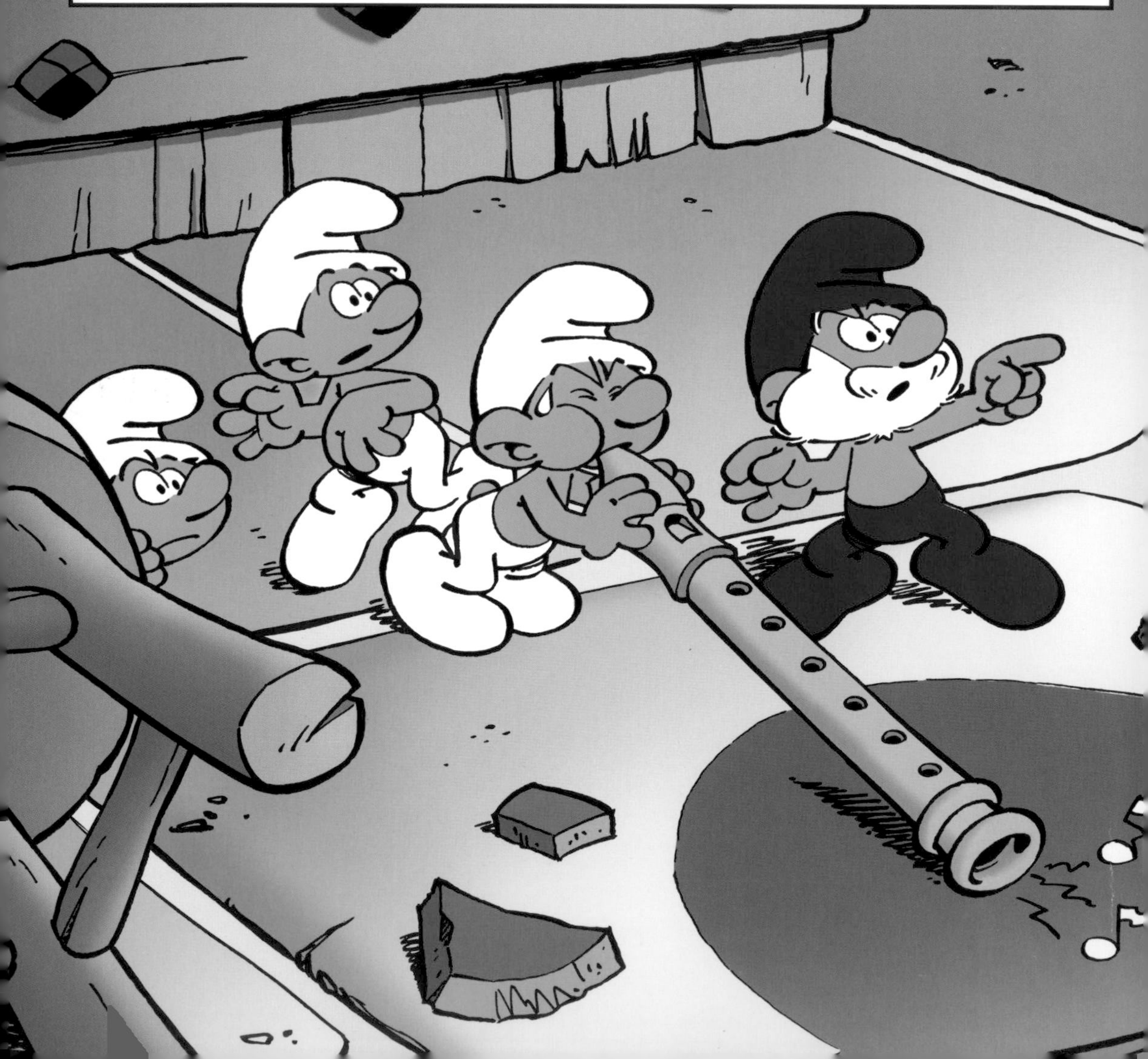

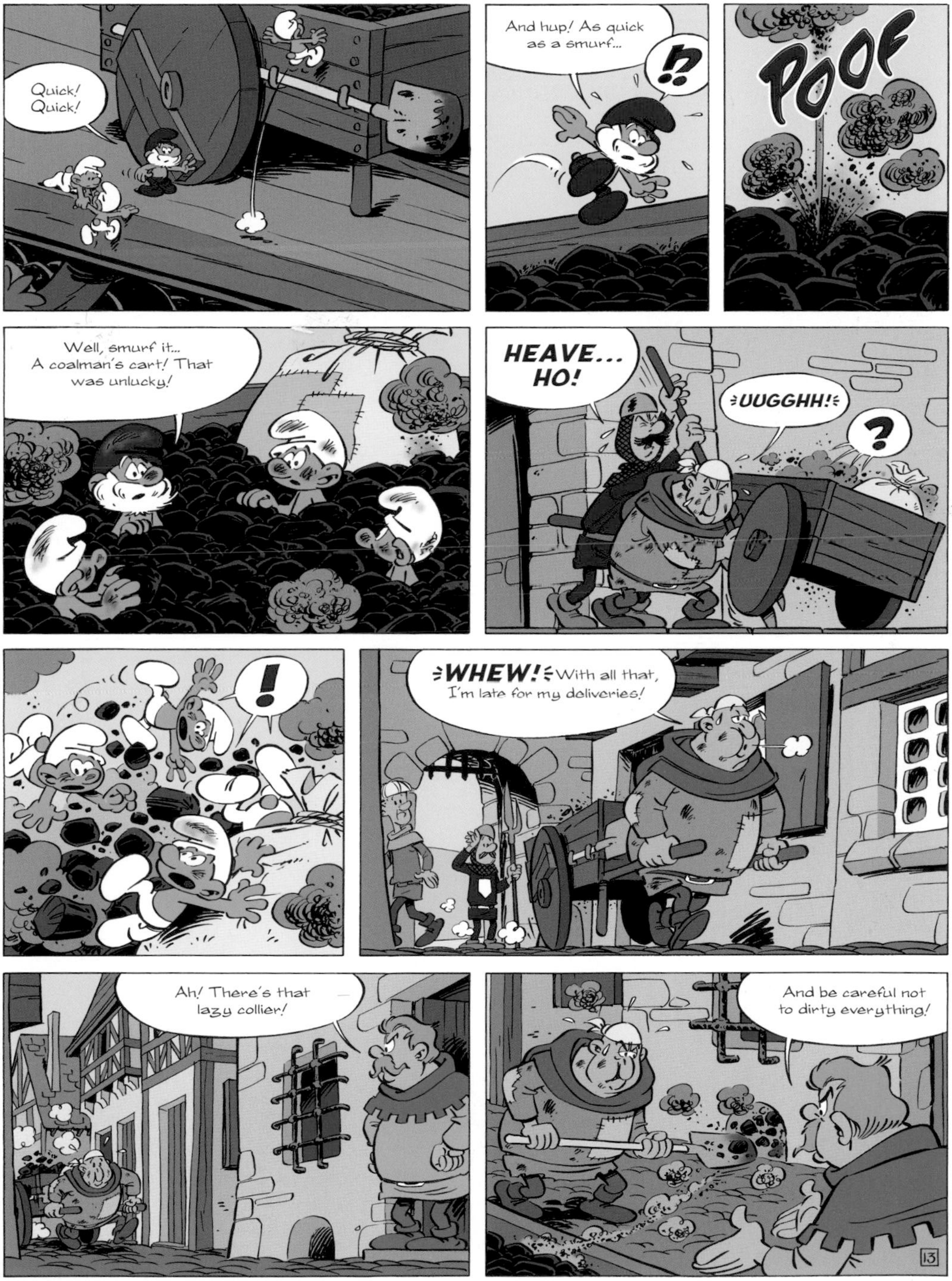
Quick! Quick!
And hup! As quick as a smurf...
!?
POOF
Well, smurf it... A coalman's cart! That was unlucky!
HEAVE... HO!
UUGGHH!
?
!
WHEW! With all that, I'm late for my deliveries!
Ah! There's that lazy collier!
And be careful not to dirty everything!
13

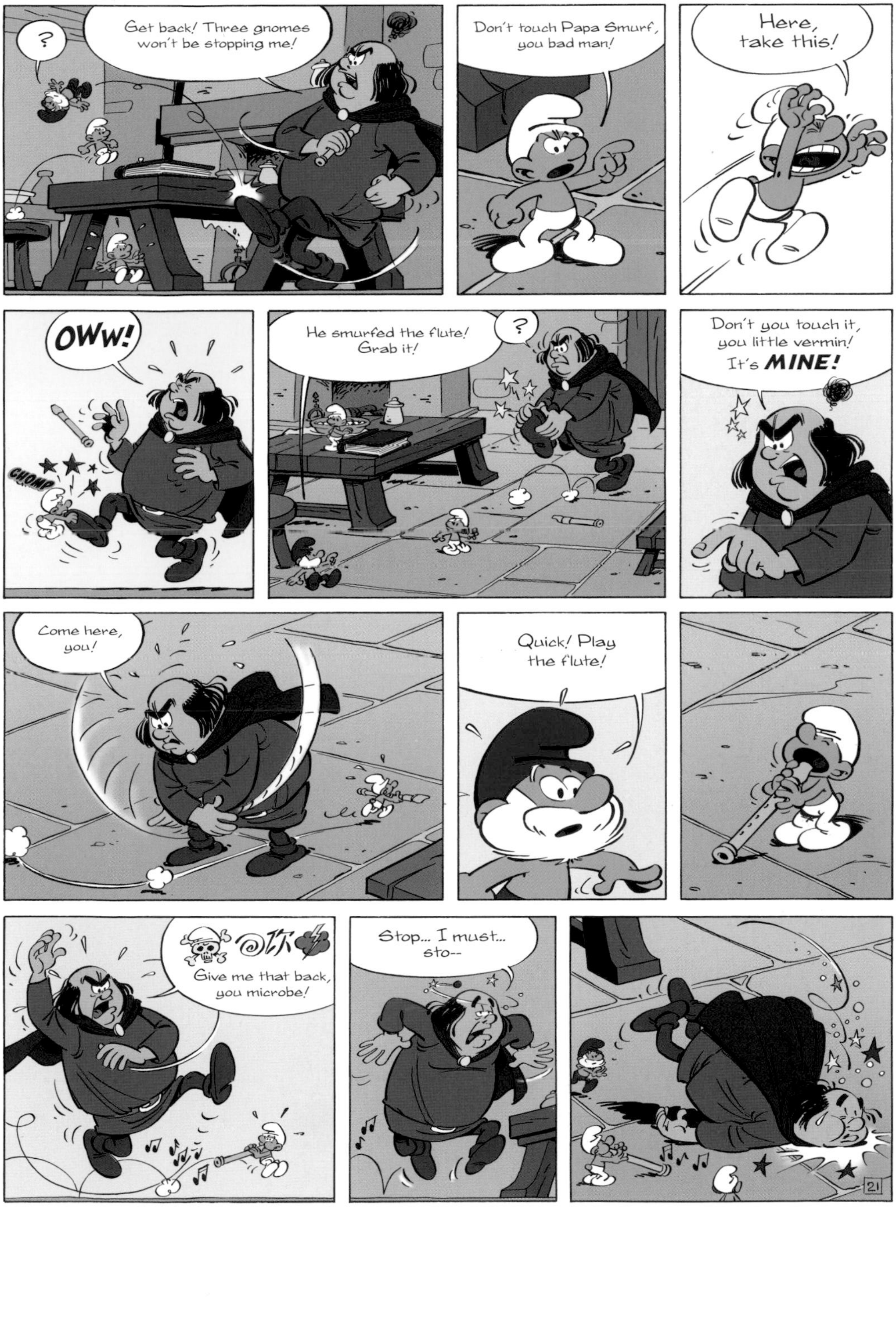
?
Get back! Three gnomes won't be stopping me!
Don't touch Papa Smurf, you bad man!
Here, take this!
OWW!
CHOMP
He smurfed the flute! Grab it!
?
Don't you touch it, you little vermin! It's MINE!
Come here, you!
Quick! Play the flute!
Give me that back, you microbe!
Stop... I must... sto--
21

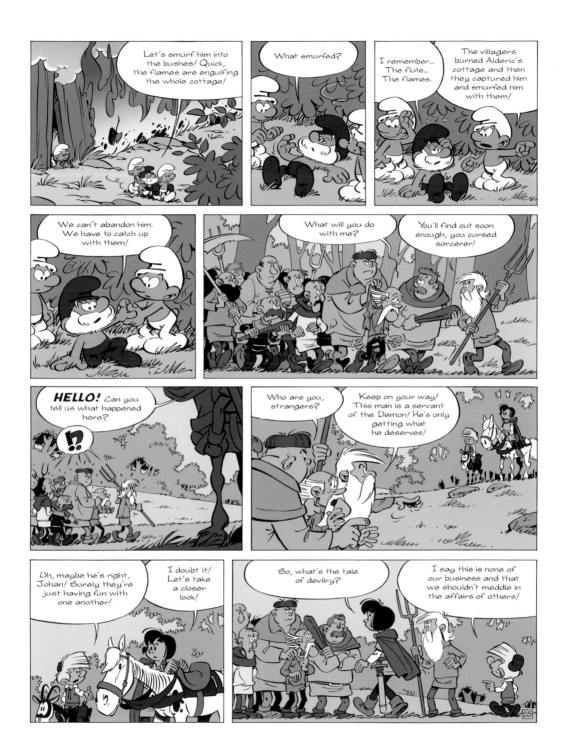

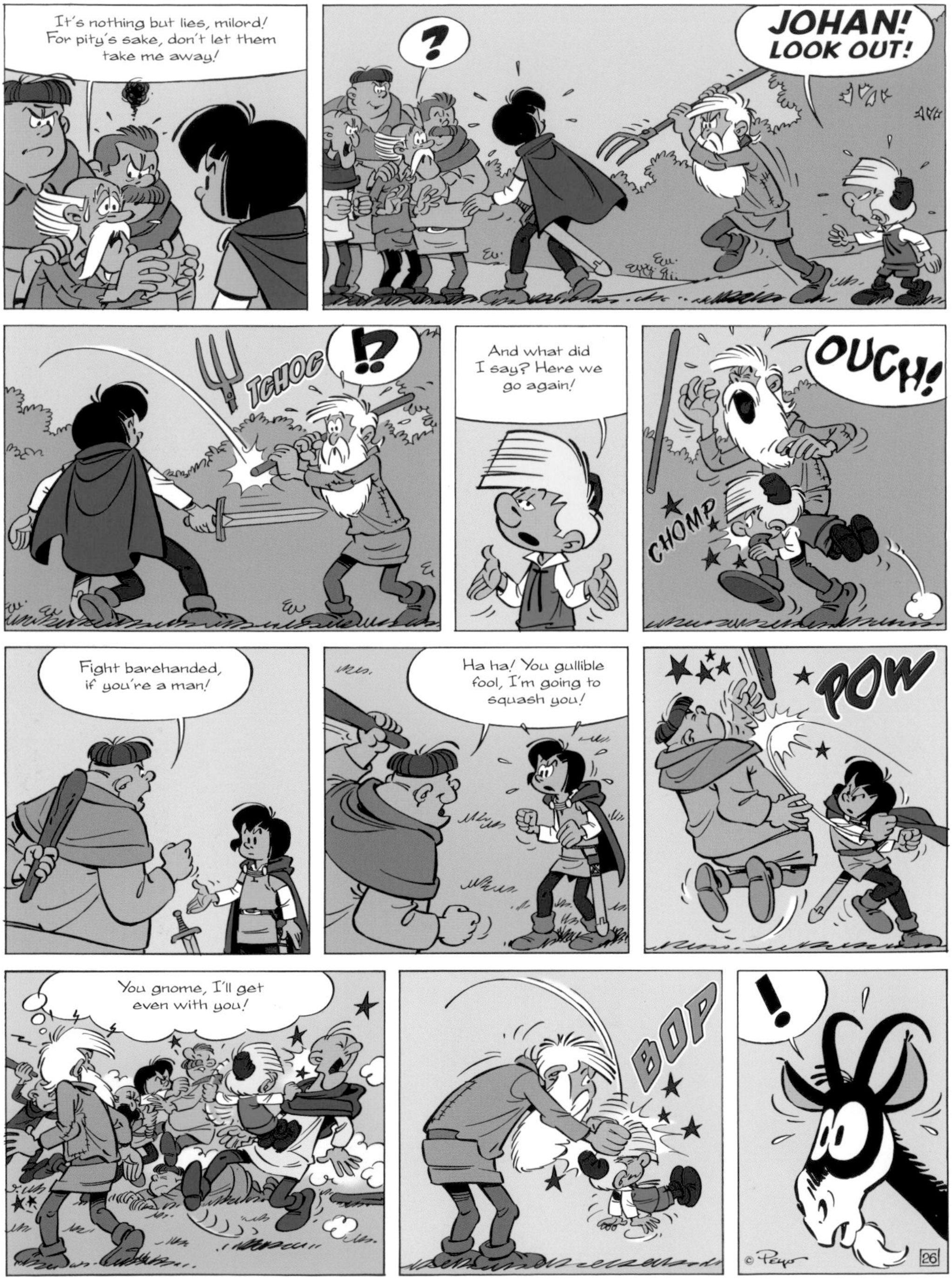
It's nothing but lies, milord! For pity's sake, don't let them take me away!
?
JOHAN! LOOK OUT!
TCHOC
!?
And what did I say? Here we go again!
OUCH!
CHOMP
Fight barehanded, if you're a man!
Ha ha! You gullible fool, I'm going to squash you!
POW
You gnome, I'll get even with you!
BOP
!
© Peyo
26

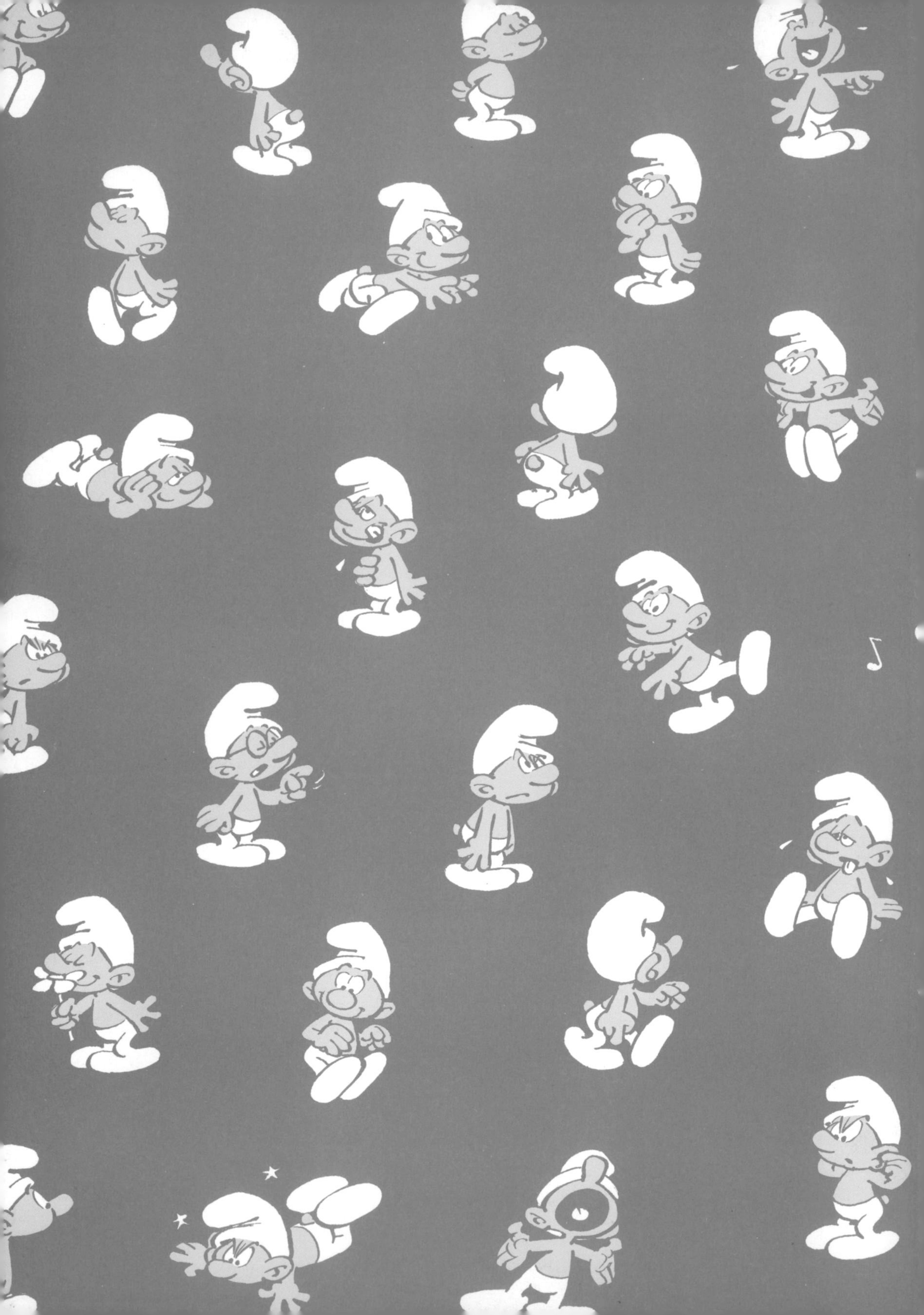